# FROM LANGUAGE TO LANGUAGE

**Also by Souleymane Bachir Diagne**

*African Art as Philosophy:*
*Senghor, Bergson, and the Idea of Negritude*

# *From* LANGUAGE *to* LANGUAGE

◆

*The Hospitality of Translation*

◆

**Souleymane Bachir Diagne**

*Translated from the French by Dylan Temel*

OTHER PRESS | NEW YORK

Originally published in French as *De langue à langue: L'hospitalité de la traduction*
in 2022 by Éditions Albin Michel, Paris



Production editor: Yvonne E. Cárdenas
Text designer: Patrice Sheridan
This book was set in Minion Pro and Bauer Bodoni by
Alpha Design & Composition of Pittsfield, NH

1 3 5 7 9 10 8 6 4 2

 Printed in the United States of America on acid-free paper. For information write to Other Press LLC, 267 Fifth Avenue, 6th Floor, New York, NY 10016. Or visit our Web site: www.otherpress.com

Library of Congress Cataloging-in-Publication Data
Names: Diagne, Souleymane Bachir author | Temel, Dylan translator
Title: From language to language : the hospitality of translation /
Souleymane Bachir Diagne ; translated from the French by Dylan Temel.
Other titles: De langue a langue. English
Description: New York : Other Press, 2025. | "Originally published in French as
De langue a langue: L'hospitalité de la traduction in 2022 by Editions
Albin Michel, Paris"—Title page verso. | Includes bibliographical references.
Identifiers: LCCN 2025412015 (print) | LCCN 2025002174 (ebook) |
ISBN 9781635423938 hardcover | ISBN 9781635423945 ebook
Subjects: LCSH: Translating and interpreting—Philosophy
Classification: LCC P306.2 .D52413 2025 (print) | LCC P306.2 (ebook) |
DDC 418/.0201—dc23/eng/20250519
LC record available at https://lccn.loc.gov/2025412015
LC ebook record available at https://lccn.loc.gov/2025002174

To understand the other,
we must not annex it
but become its host.

—LOUIS MASSIGNON

# PREFACE TO THE ENGLISH-LANGUAGE EDITION

◆

IN 2002 WE—MY WIFE, Mariame, our four children, and I—left Senegal to settle in Chicago, where we had decided to make a life for ourselves. Since 1999, I had been shuttling back and forth between Chicago and Senegal every year to give a quarterly course at Northwestern University from March to the end of May, after having taught philosophy for one semester, from October to the end of February, at Cheikh Anta Diop University in Dakar. But now I was not just teaching on a temporary basis each term before going back home. Home was Chicago, where I was a full-time full professor in the Departments of Philosophy, Religion, and African Studies at Northwestern. With Mariame; our eldest son, age thirteen; our twin boys, age eleven; and our daughter, age five, we now had to love our new life, integrate ourselves into the Windy City and its culture, come to terms with its endless winters and snowstorms, and, since we lived on the North Side, share with our fellow Chicagoans both the misery of always seeing the Cubs baseball team lose and the ability to keep faith in the outcome of the following season.[1]

Above all, we had to cherish and maintain our multilingualism now that the English language was going to be dominant in our lives. Luckily, we were able to enroll the children in a program called École Franco-Américaine de Chicago (EFAC), housed at Abraham Lincoln Elementary School with an extension at Lincoln Park High School in the same neighborhood. Thanks to this program, they were able to remain perfectly francophone. And even though our children quickly got used to speaking to one another in English, Mariame was adamant about maintaining Wolof at home. And there were also the family vacations in Senegal to anchor the use of the language, which did not have the support of school education. Then there were the Arabic script and language that our children were introduced to through the learning of the Quran. They had reasons to be proud of living between many languages.

One day, shortly after we had settled in Chicago, our family was faced with the very question of pride in speaking our native tongue. We were quietly enjoying burgers and fries at a Burger King near Northwestern's campus in the suburb of Evanston, speaking in Wolof with occasional incursions of French. A woman and her three children were sitting next to us. At a certain point, the children, who were about the same age as my boys, started to make fun of us, pretending to speak "like us" with guttural sounds that made them laugh: a way of saying that our language was not really one. I expected their mother to ask them to stop and maybe even make the moment an opportunity to teach her progeny something about the diversity and equality of languages and cultures. I guess I was being naive. The mother, unperturbed, continued to consider her burger the most important thing in the world, simply waiting for her children to move on. Which they soon did.

It was up to Mariame and me to make sure that the lesson the Burger King woman had failed to draw for her children from that moment would be understood by our own. Basically, the kids who had seen it as funny to "imitate" what appeared to them a barbaric sub-language had merely demonstrated, with the innocence of their age, the fact, in the words of linguist John McWhorter, that "when a language works so differently from ours, a natural gut-level impression is that it is a departure from normality."[2] When we made the decision to move to the United States, one of our concerns was that our children would now be living as a "minority" in their new country. It was essential that they live out their different identities and the languages that expressed them with self-assurance and pride. It was important for them to understand that Wolof was just as valuable as Anglo-American English, which they would soon be speaking along with the kids who had thought they had to make fun of our language—but with the advantage of being able to look at the world from the viewpoint of other languages.

In a way, this book continues the lesson contained in that moment at the Burger King in Evanston. Two main theses underlie the arguments presented in it. The first is that all human languages are of equal value. The second is that nothing manifests this equivalence better than translation. And I could add a conclusion drawn from the theses, which is ultimately the message of this book: that translation is a humanism. There are, of course, many reasons to be surprised that translation can be presented as a manifestation of the equivalence of our idioms. Indeed, a sociopolitical approach to translation is quick to remind us of the inequality of languages, by immediately establishing a hierarchy among those that are the most translated or receive the most works in translation. And at the heart of the so-called postcolonial turn in translation studies is the notion that translation is often linked to colonialism, revealing its symbolic violence.

What this book says is that the truth of translation must be read through a phenomenological approach to the ethical disposition in which translators find themselves when they bring into contact two languages, one of which gives hospitality to what has been thought and created in the other. What they then experience in this side-by-side encounter is that, while translation certainly has to deal with the untranslatable, what Édouard Glissant calls "opacity," it manifests, ultimately, the truth expressed in the subtitle of McWhorter's book *The Language Hoax*, that "the world looks the same in any language," and his view of the "magnificence of how a language," *any language*, "is built."

*Language to Language*, celebrating the hospitality of translation, is an exploration of that experience.

*Souleymane Bachir Diagne*
*New York City, October 29, 2024*

# INTRODUCTION: TRANSLATION AGAINST DOMINATION

◆

> The essence of translation is to be an opening, a dialogue, a crossbreeding, a decentering. Translation is "a putting in touch with," or it is nothing.[1]
>
> —ANTOINE BERMAN

ON JANUARY 20, 2021, the entire world was fixed to their television screens, watching the inauguration of the forty-sixth president of the United States. The attention naturally given to such a global event as a new American president's installation was compounded by a set of circumstances that rendered the swearing in of Joe Biden and Kamala Harris an exceptional moment. We were still, and once again, in the worst of the pandemic and mere weeks before had witnessed, in utter astonishment, an attack by far-right extremists, including white supremacists, on the Capitol. Democracy was shaken to its core.

Something vital was at play on the esplanade of that very Capitol, where the new president was to declare that "democracy [had] prevailed." In the midst of a pandemic, it was, of course, impossible for a large audience to crowd the stage to celebrate this triumph of democracy, for a communion of minds and bodies to bear witness to one of the essential values of our modernity, whose very fragility and preciousness were made manifest by the assault upon it. All the more necessary, then, for one moment to symbolize and capture the meaning of it all. This moment came in the form of a poem that left even the sun standing still.

Amanda Gorman recited "The Hill We Climb."

It was only natural that the following days saw a rush of proposals seeking to translate this moment that the entire world had experienced live, to spread and share its magic in an array of languages. Such projects remind us that translation is the expression, in the language that welcomes it, of an unmitigated love, often at first sight, for something created in another one. Indeed, Antoine Berman tells us that translating is an "experience," suggesting the meaning that Heidegger gives to this word, as he writes that "to undergo an experience with something... means that this something befalls us, strikes us, comes over us, overwhelms and transforms us."[2]

Among the various projects that would allow us to "undergo an experience," in other languages, with Amanda Gorman's poem, that of the Dutch publisher Meulenhoff would soon give rise to a dispute that would reignite, and with much ado, heated debates around what it means to translate and who has the authority to do so. The publisher sought to put out a collection of Gorman's poetry centered around "The Hill We Climb" and decided to entrust its translation to the Dutch poet Marieke Lucas Rijneveld. The latter ultimately decided to decline what they had initially welcomed as an "honor" once the project was subjected to a vociferous media frenzy, the likes of which we know all too well: they were accused of ignoring the fact that the task of reconstituting the "experience" of Amanda Gorman's poetry should be conferred upon a translator sharing her same "experience" of being, in the words of Janice Deul, "a young woman, a spoken word artist, and unapologetically Black."[3]

It is undoubtedly necessary to fight for the recognition and representation of marginalized groups so that publishing, in all its sectors, and especially in translation, creates space for talented minority writers. One may likewise grant that a translation of Amanda Gorman's poetry would be a good opportunity to invite, for one, such minorities to receive the "honor" that was given to Marieke Lucas Rijneveld and to consider, moreover, that beyond the requisite linguistic competencies in the source and target languages, they would bring the richness of a certain "experience" tied to their identities to the enterprise of translation.

The fact remains that the tone and terms in which the controversy played out did not allow for a genuine interrogation of the relationship between the lived "experience" of certain identities and the "experience" one undergoes with a poem. Other decisions were certainly made, as we know, in light of the Dutch controversy and so as to avoid repeating it: while for some languages, the translation of "The Hill We Climb" was entrusted to people who share certain facets of Amanda Gorman's identities—plural, as for all of us—for others, publishers called upon "multicultural" teams. Which raises the question of whether the (political, it must be said) expediency of making translation the work of teams that collaborate and share a collective responsibility would not in fact dissolve the singular experience of love at first sight and the difficulty of reproducing this sensation, like an echo, in another language, which is precisely the task of the translator. A team to climb the hill of translating a burdensome technical work is understandable. But a poem?

Should translations prioritize alleged similarities between the author and translator, which supposedly render transmission from the former to the latter that much easier, or rather the state of disorientation that is the inevitable condition of translating? Those who make no claims to knowledge, but rather accept that they will find themselves in unknown territory when they decide to translate a text that they love all the same, are those who will be able to, in the words of Christine Lombez, "give the poem the chance to be what it inherently is, abandoning the mold that would force it into an awkward and ill-fitting contortion."[4]

This book presents a reflection on translation and its capacity, its power to create relations of equivalence and reciprocity between identities, to make them coexist, that is to say, exist together on equal footing, such that from language to language we can speak with and understand each other. As Antoine Berman writes, translation is a putting in touch with or it is nothing. This text is, then, "in praise of translation" and invites the reader to consider it as a "humanism," expressing an optimistic vision of what it can accomplish.[5]

Optimism is not naiveté.

It is more than evident, to allude to the subtitle of Pascale Casanova's book on the global sociology and politics of translation, *La langue mondiale* [The global language], that indeed, this word rhymes with "domination"[6]—we must recognize the reality of a "linguistic marketplace" that distributes human languages into such categories as "peripheral languages, central languages, hypercentral languages, and the hypercentral language."[7] Such a distribution has consequences not only for the relative "prestige" of these languages and therefore the cultures they embody, but also for their very existence. Languages die, as does, along with them, their unique outlook on the human condition. And if they disappear, it is because they find themselves on the periphery of a more "central" language, a lingua franca that absorbs them bit by bit. The existence of a hierarchy of languages and relations of domination among languages is a fact that any reflection on a humanism of translation must take into account.

In her book, Pascale Casanova repeatedly returns, first, to the assessment that one essential form linguistic domination may take, which constitutes the measure of it, is diglossia, defined as a bilingual situation in which one language is considered to be inferior and endowed with a lesser cultural capital. Therefore, it is never recognized or employed for scholarly or socially prestigious uses.[8] Another important observation is that, when carried out from a more "peripheral" language toward a more "central" one, translation represents an increase in value. Conversely, to receive in one's language, by way of translation, what was conceived and created in the "hypercentral language," let's say English to call it what it is, is to become augmented from its essence.

Calling to mind the work of Gisèle Sapiro,[9] which brings our attention to the increasingly influential domination of English in the economy and politics of linguistic exchange, Casanova demonstrates that translation most often takes place in a context of asymmetry of the languages in question. Either it "raises up" minor idioms closer toward the center, to a state of *plus being*, or, on the contrary, it leads them to gather, like an offering, the surplus of being that the central language thereby grants to the periphery.

How, then, could we think that translation is able to go against asymmetry and domination in order to build reciprocity?

Analyzing translation as the embodiment of linguistic domination likewise points toward the possibility of seeing within it a "resisting force." "There is but one way," writes Casanova, "to effectively combat the domination of a language, which is to adopt an 'atheistic' position, and thus not to *believe* in the prestige of said language, to be persuaded that its authority and domination are entirely arbitrary."[10]

Let us consider the most asymmetrical situation there is, the colonial situation. Generally speaking, an imperial language imposes itself as the incarnation of the Logos, the perfect language of a fully realized humanity, relative to which indigenous ways of speaking are incomplete and defined by what they *lack*. A lack of abstract concepts, a lack of future tenses, and finally, perhaps above all, a lack of the verb *to be*.[11]

In regions that have experienced colonization or that still do, there live, to borrow Pascale Casanova's definition, "those who, collectively, use two languages" because they "are the dominated." Their world is therefore one of diglossia, in which everything leads them to accept and believe that one of their languages, the one said to be "native," has essentially less value than the other, whose natural "prestige" thereby legitimizes its domination. Ceasing to believe in this prestige and realizing, on the contrary, that any language is worth as much as another, because it is but one among many, can take two forms. The first is a linguistic nationalism that manifests itself by rejecting the "dominant" language after the aura surrounding it has dissipated. The second is a movement from diglossia toward true bilingualism (or, certainly, multilingualism).

Thus, one of the very first acts of Léopold Sédar Senghor's Négritude was to proclaim, against colonial diglossia, that the future lies in bilingualism and in the "new man" who thinks from language to language.[12] This came in the 1937 lecture that the colonial administration established in Dakar had invited him to give at the city's chamber of commerce.[13]

To praise translation is not to ignore that it is domination. It is to celebrate the plurality of languages and their equality. It is to be opposed to inscribing translation into a world of unequal exchange, to remember that the objective of translation, of the task of the translator, of their ethic and poetics, is precisely to create reciprocity and encounters within a common humanity. It is to say that, against the asymmetry of colonialism, it is a decolonizing force, and against economy, it is charity.

# 1.

# THE LINGUIST, THE NATIVE, AND THE EXTRATERRESTRIAL

◆

> The common sense behind the maxim is that one's interlocutor's silliness, beyond a certain point, is less likely than a bad translation.[1]
>
> —WILLARD VAN ORMAN QUINE

THE THOUGHT EXPERIMENT THAT Willard Van Orman Quine (1908–2000) conceived of as "radical translation"[2] appears at first glance to represent the situation of colonial asymmetry, before ultimately affirming our equality and proclaiming a shared human identity.

Let us recall what it means for a translation to be "radical."

In order to understand the bonds that constitute our life in society, we should proceed, suggest Thomas Hobbes and Jean-Jacques Rousseau, from a "fictional" state before society, a state of nature: that is to say, we should examine the reasons for and mechanisms by which we left this state in order to understand the one that follows it, thereby reaching the meaning of the social contract. In the same way, in order to understand the language we use to communicate, we should begin with a "fictional" state before language so as to examine the reasons, or rather, the emotions, per Rousseau, that compelled us to sing what we mean prior to articulating our words.[3] This sort of philosophical fiction, which allows us to get to the heart of an issue, is what Quine develops in order to understand what it is to understand. Which is to say, to translate, if we are to view "understanding as translation," as suggests the title George Steiner gave to the very first chapter of his book *After Babel*.[4]

Thus Quine imagines a fictional state of total incomprehension of the other's language by the subject in question, an initial state from which he must methodically come to establish a glossary allowing him to translate the foreign language into his own. We are invited to imagine someone possessed by a curiosity for the most foreign cultural forms possible, and thus for languages radically different from those with which he could have even the slightest acquaintance.

Quine insists upon an utter lack of common ground, upon the absolute disorientation of the subject, and upon the blank slate from which he must establish a translation manual of the other's language. This absence of any point of reference is not only a result of the foreignness of the other's speech; even though English and Hungarian are not related in the slightest (as opposed to "kindred languages," such as Frisian and English), translation between them may nevertheless "be aided by traditional equations that have evolved in step with a shared culture."[5]

## THE LINGUIST AND THE NATIVE

Consequently, the subject of the inquiry is to be an ethnologist and a linguist in one. And rightly so, for here he has discovered "a hitherto untouched people"[6] whose language bears no resemblance to anything he could possibly recognize. He must therefore also be a behaviorist, because, for this undertaking, all he has at his disposal is the other's behavior, that is to say his responses/reactions, and particularly the verbal ones, to what happens around them. Moreover, according to Quine, in linguistics, as far as language acquisition is concerned, one has no choice but to be a behaviorist.[7]

As we can see, the fiction fits perfectly into the ethnological framework, both in terms of the language of the asymmetrical encounter between the subject who is from "our civilization," and who therefore *is supposed to know*, and the native, whose language, we should not be surprised to learn, is quite naturally called "Jungle."[8] Crucially, this asymmetry signifies that between the linguist and the native, there is simply no interlocution. Granted, when one designs such a philosophical fiction to give an account of meaning as it emerges from a zero degree, one may dispose of any hypotheses as one pleases. Nevertheless, no initiative on the part of the speaker of "Jungle" comes from his will to help the foreigner (at the end of the day, he, in the eyes of the "native," becomes the foreigner) to understand him. Understanding and translating are one-sided.

The native, then, is simply tasked with offering his reactions to the stimuli produced by different situations and circumstances. The famous example of a stimulus-response pair that Quine presents first is that of a rabbit appearing, which leads the native to say the word (but is it just one word?) *gavagai*. It is clear that this utterance may have several meanings tied in various ways to the appearance of a rabbit. The linguist therefore has to elicit additional elements from his informant (and we must take care not to impart upon this word even the slightest agency) in order to settle on, say, "rabbit!" or "Lo, a rabbit!" He can move forward only through conjecture, tentative confirmation, and/or refutation.

Consequently, he must quickly identify the two responses corresponding to "yes" and "no," to assent and dissent, for the native. To identify them with absolute certainty would require a whole litany of tests, for there is no reason to posit the existence of a universal system of body language or set of gestures signifying "yes" and "no." Indeed, Quine suggests as a counterexample the gestures of Turkish body language, which are, in his words, "nearly the reverse of our own."[9]

Having performed the requisite tests, the linguist comes to identify *evet* for "yes" and *yok* for "no." He has likewise begun to gather utterances in Jungle that he could reasonably consider to be observational, in other words, that "cling" in a direct way to a state of things observable by all. He could then consider the possibility of translating utterances formed using the binary connectives "and," "or," "but," or the unary "not" for negation. Generally speaking, without going into further detail on the comprehension/translation of Jungle, we can say that the ethnolinguist will make use of analytical hypotheses and guesswork, with "more extravagant guesswork to follow," Quine adds, in order to establish "a tentative Jungle vocabulary, with English translations, and a tentative apparatus of grammatical constructions."[10]

The tentative nature of the translation manual such as it is established here is not fated to disappear in a definitive work to come later on. It is in its nature to be forever tentative, forever open, and continuously subject to the reactions its usage provokes from the natives. Its open and tentative nature similarly leads us to one of the main conclusions to arise from the experiment at hand: we can imagine perfectly well that the manual established by another ethnolinguist, going about the same process, would be just as effective in terms of the assenting responses that his hypotheses provoke. Therein lies Quine's thesis of the "indeterminacy of translation," which he formulates as follows:

> [Our] reflections leave us little reason to expect that two radical translators, working independently on Jungle, would come out with interchangeable manuals. Their manuals might be indistinguishable in terms of any native behavior that they give reason to expect, and yet each manual might prescribe some translations that the other translator would reject. Such is the thesis of indeterminacy of translation.[11]

We have good reason to believe that there must be something invariable at the core of these two manuals such that they are both practicable for the same language and, first and foremost, achievable. Namely, something must be exempt from indeterminacy: that something is logic.

The question, generally speaking, of the universality of logic as the grammar of reasoning, not bound to any specific grammar of different human languages, is ancient. The translation into Arabic, for instance, of the works comprising Aristotle's *Organon*, which was considered to be the universal instrument (*organon* in Greek) of valid reasoning, thus raised the question of the relationship between Aristotle's logic and the Stagirite's Greek.[12] In the seventeenth century, Gottfried Wilhelm Leibniz pursued this project of translating our processes of reasoning into a language whose grammar was to be "philosophically" reconstituted so as to be solely that of our understanding, of our capacity to reason and to come to conclusions, not distorted by the ambiguities and uncertainties of natural language. This language, for him, was algebra.

This project of an algebra of logic was to be given further shape by the English mathematician George Boole (1815–1864). Boole's intention was to revive the Leibnizian idea of a language of algebraic "characters" that did not represent quantities as in ordinary algebra, but rather, the concepts that we put together in our speech and reasoning. The operators of combination themselves could therefore be expressed by the usual algebraic symbols of addition, multiplication, etcetera without, of course, having any quantitative meaning attached to them. Equality would have the value of identity.

Boole, like Leibniz, believed that this *lingua characteristica universalis*, this universal symbolic language in which our reasoning would take the form of a calculation obeying the rules of nonnumerical algebra, was the expression of something invariable lying beneath the infinite diversity of human languages—the Adamic language, common to all humans before the catastrophe of Babel.

Regarding the idea of an invariable "Adamic" logic, it is worth citing, in addition to Boole, another author who was behind profound revolutions in the field of logic after Leibniz: Gottlob Frege (1848–1925).

Boole takes as fact that there subsists the same atavistic foundation within all human speech. He declares, in fact, that it would be difficult for us to "conceive that the unnumbered tongues and dialects of the earth should have preserved through a long succession of ages so much that is common and universal, were we not assured of the existence of some deep foundation of their agreement in the laws of the mind itself."[13]

As for Frege, he begins by saying that grammar is to our language as logic is to our thought, that grammar is "a mix of logic and psychology." If nothing psychological crept in, if our grammars were logic through and through, they would necessarily be the same for all languages, Frege adds, continuing as follows:

> Can the same thought be expressed in different languages? Without a doubt, so far as the logical kernel is concerned; for otherwise it would not be possible for human beings to share a common intellectual life. But if we think of the kernel with the psychological husk added, a precise translation is impossible. Indeed we may go so far as to doubt whether the outer covering is the same for any two men. From this we can see the value of learning foreign languages for one's logical education . . . This is how differences between languages can facilitate our grasp of what is logical.[14]

The skeptical behavioralist in Quine refrains from taking it as *fact* that the "tongues and dialects of the earth" are all bound by an "agreement" built on laws that exist in the mind, which are in turn reflected in the signs we use to communicate. Moreover, his very approach consists in not taking as a given, a priori, thoughts whose translation into different languages would be a mere change of their outer shell. In this way he follows neither Boole nor Frege.

Translation is not mediated by some pure language. It is carried out directly, from Jungle to English, from language to language. The difficulty lies, then, as was recognized by Quine and highlighted in the objections that were addressed to him, in explaining why "that which is logical" is exempt from indeterminacy. The question does not fall within the bounds of the thought experiment, which is concerned with the creation of a translation manual, but transcends it in the sense that it extends to the very condition of possibility of the enterprise of translating. We therefore must proceed from the principle that "that which is logical," and which imposes itself on us when we speak English, likewise imposes itself on the speakers of Jungle.

How can we justify this decision, since it is indeed a decision? Why not decide, on the contrary, that the speaker of a radically foreign language likewise thinks according to a logic entirely different from "our" classical logic, based on the laws of identity, contradiction, and excluded middle? These questions go beyond the plane of the thought experiment, as they are *practical* both in the sense that, on one hand, they require an empirical response and, on the other, they lead us from a *logic* to an *ethics* of translation.

Pure philosophical fiction must now give way to anthropology. Sandra Laugier reminds us that discussions of the notion of "radical translation" tend to focus on techniques of establishing the translation manual and overlook a key issue, namely, the anthropological status of logic.[15] Indeed, in order to justify the decision not to attribute "that which is logical" to Jungle, the real world of these animals-who-speak that are humans must be able to provide examples of peoples who express themselves in total indifference to the principle of noncontradiction, for example, and who would thus display a mentality that was non-logical, or "pre-logical," per Lucien Lévy-Bruhl's concept.

Quine's thought experiment of radical translation could not go without questioning a certain ethnology, Lévy-Bruhl's in particular, and his *decision* to posit that the mentality he calls "primitive" does not function according to the same laws as "our" thinking and that consequently, its speech cannot truly be translated into that of "our" civilization. It is necessary to speak here of a *decision*, that is to say, a disposition to consider a priori that we are dealing with an alternative logic. If we find this to be so, it is because we proceeded from the principle that it necessarily must be so.

We must also remember that the elder Levy-Bruhl's ethnological decision to see an untranslatable prelogicality within the "primitive mentality" is an extension of his philosophical decision to challenge the idea of "a humanity always and everywhere exactly like itself."[16] "The Greeks," he continues, citing Hegel, "knew Greece, they did not know humanity."[17] For them, the division between the Logos and the languages of the barbarians signified a fracture between the finite world of the Greek cities and the rest of human beings inhabiting the indefinite, "*τὸ ἄπειρον*."[18] It was Christianity, he continues, which, moved by a proselytical impulse altogether foreign to the Ancients, proceeded to erase the difference between Romans and Greeks on one hand and barbarians on the other, as between the chosen people and the Gentiles. Based on the biblical story of Adam, who implicates all of mankind in his fall, and Christ, who redeems them, this religion created the illusion "that Christian humanity and humanity in general were almost the same thing."[19]

Philosophers have only kept up this very same illusion, which has become a "deep-rooted belief," Lévy-Bruhl goes on, by turning the foreign peoples who were the subjects of their inquiries into "thinly disguised Europeans."[20]

However, according to him, the facts empirically established by history and anthropology opposed that confused notion of *a* humanity, upon which is founded the notion of a natural and universal morality, and increasingly so. Indeed, he believed that these social sciences demonstrate that "humanity as one whole... is merely a united collection";[21] that "inferior societies no longer lend themselves merely to a facile antithesis between the corrupted European and the 'noble savage,'" but that they are radically other, with a mentality dominated by a *logic of images* and a *logic of feelings* that lead them to take up beliefs and adopt practices that cannot be explained by "our" logic.

In reality, rather than stemming from empirically established facts, the philosophical decision to see the other as radically other goes a step ahead of the given information by bending it and expecting it to verify the non-logical nature of the "primitive mentality" and thus its radical untranslatability in our language created by logic. An ethnology of difference stems from this decision.

Against this, are we simply to propose an ethnology of identity?

As good skeptics, says Quine, we must recognize that we cannot choose between two *decisions* on a theoretical basis, just like that.

> I am not sure that it even makes sense to ask. We may alternately wonder at the inscrutability of the native mind and wonder at how very much like us the native is, where in the one case we have merely muffled the best translation and in the other case we have done a more thorough job of reading our own provincial modes into the native's speech.[22]

The right decision to make is therefore dictated by a "practical morality," Quine writes, which will express first and foremost a skepticism toward the impulse to establish certain "cultural contrasts" that motivate the ethnologist of difference. Thus, when he claims that "certain natives are said to accept as true certain sentences translatable in the form '*p* and not *p*,'"[23] in other words, that their mentality is perfectly accommodated to the possibility that something could be itself and its opposite at the same time and in the same respect, he demonstrates that he is simply a bad translator of the sentence in question, victim as he is of his own predisposition to find himself in the face of a "primitive's" illogicality.

To speak of a "practical morality" rather than tossing out both the ethnology of difference and that of identity is to shift the question of translation toward an ethical plane.[24] In this way, Quine puts forth the *principle* of considering the native as being rational and logical, that we can always translate their language, however foreign it may be from ours, and that from language to language we can always understand each other.

It truly is a principle and not a thesis that can be arrived at over the course of a demonstration. It is in this regard that the American philosopher uses the word *empathy* and the expression "principle of charity."[25] Both express the idea of gratitude and equality within a shared humanity, which is at the very heart of translation. We must clarify here that the word *charity* must be understood in the etymological sense, including its religious connotation of identification with the other. In this way the thought experiment that at first had every trace of a colonial ethnology is revealed to be an affirmation that translation is a "putting in touch with."

There are two primary reasons to adopt a principle of charity rather than an ethnology of contrast.

The first, which bears repeating, is that the latter, by its very nature, perverts any translation by expecting it at all costs to be foreign. In doing so, it forgets that one can always fabricate, through "perversity" (to use Quine's word), the foreign out of the familiar. This is the lesson that such an ethnology should retain from Montesquieu's *Persian Letters*, in which he playfully turns the very customs of his own society into aberrant behaviors by having them observed by outsiders.

The second, and crucial, reason is that this principle is not only applied when learning a foreign language, but also in play when children learn to speak what will become their so-called mother tongue. Just like the ethnolinguist, their hesitation when repeating words and phrases shows how attuned they are to the assent they hope for from those around them. They learn to translate behaviors into speech because they learn that in doing so, they enter, through empathy, a community.

## THE LINGUIST AND THE EXTRATERRESTRIAL

Generally speaking, to translate is to create human community with the speakers of the language that one is translating. We might well then ask, with an ounce of perversity: What about with nonhumans?

This is the question raised rhetorically by Sandra Laugier and Denis Bonnay when, in their reading of Quine's thought experiment, they make the following remark: "After all, our societies would provide numerous examples of contradictions if they were looked upon by a curious extraterrestrial anthropologist."[26] And indeed, science fiction has taken thought experiments of this kind as one of its favorite premises.

The shortcut of resorting to telepathic communication, a common theme in the genre, allows us to ignore or bypass the issue of translation. Certain works have become classics, however, for, among other reasons, tackling head-on the challenge of imagining credible solutions to the problem of translating *in spite of everything*, or in spite of the a priori impossibility thereof. This challenge is what accounts for the poetry of such magnificent films as Steven Spielberg's *Close Encounters of the Third Kind* (1977) and Denis Villeneuve's *Arrival* (2016). Whereas in the former, humans and aliens have recourse to the supposedly "universal" medium of musical notes and colors, in the latter, the experience of translation and mutual understanding is imagined from language to language.

*Arrival* is the adaptation of "Story of Your Life,"[27] a novella by science-fiction writer Ted Chiang, who clearly conceived this fictional work likewise as a thought experiment in order to transpose questions of translation and philosophy of language into a drama.[28] These issues are generally well translated from the novella to the film, even if a number of changes are made, particularly in the way the message of the human and humanistic truth of translation is rendered, which is central to both.

Let us recall the crux of the story: visitors have arrived from beyond the stars, and we have to understand their objective.

In Chiang's novella, their spaceship stays in orbit while they establish on Earth sorts of "cabins" in order to communicate with humans. One hundred and twelve are set up, nine of which are in the United States. The story focuses in on just one of the American cabins, in which the two main characters, linguist Louise Banks and physicist Gary Donnelly (whose name becomes Ian in the film), are tasked by American (military) authorities with understanding what the aliens want and discovering whether it is possible to squeeze any knowledge or technology out of them, all while giving away as little as possible about "ours." In the cabin, communication takes place through a large window that is alternatively transparent or opaque, depending on whether the Heptapods (thus named because of their anatomy) appear on the other side.

In the film adaptation, the Heptapods place enormous spacecraft in twelve countries, on different continents, which humans have to board in order to "speak" with them. Spectators follow the adventure of translating the Heptapods' language into English from a site in Montana chosen by these visitors for North America. It is at this site that the US Army has given Louise Banks and Ian Donnelly the mission of translating the extraterrestrials' language and understanding the nature of their science.

But the other sites likewise have their own significance, as there is established from the beginning a true sense of collaboration among countries as different as the United States, Sudan, Sierra Leone, Russia, China, etcetera in order to share information gathered on the extraterrestrials' language and intentions. Inside the vessels, the same giant mirror system as in Chiang's novella allows for communication with the Heptapods, here christened Abbott and Costello by the humans (they were dubbed Flapper and Raspberry in the novella).

In the film, there is a crucial reference to the theory in cognitive anthropology known as the "Sapir-Whorf hypothesis," which essentially claims that the language we speak gives shape to the way we see the world. "Story of Your Life" does not explicitly mention this hypothesis, but it is clearly at the heart of this "fictionalization of the philosophical question" of how our categories of thought are determined by the categories of our language. It is foundational to the idea upon which the plot, in both the novella and the movie, is constructed: by teaching humans their language—which, we discover at the end, was the very goal of the journey they undertook—the Heptapods also taught them, through the intermediary of their translators, primarily Louise Banks, their perspective on what we call reality.

As she gradually allows herself to be overcome by the Heptapod language, it is revealed to the linguist that these visitors see reality as past, present, and future simultaneously. In a word, they "know" the future, and in time, learning to think in Heptapod, Louise herself also comes to know how to see the end in the beginning. When she says "yes" when the physicist Ian/Gary asks to marry her, when she says "yes" when he asks to have a child with her, she knows that she is saying "yes" to her fate, which is to have a daughter, only to watch her die at the end of adolescence—from cancer in the film, from a rock climbing accident in "Story of Your Life."

In Chiang's novella, the most explicit manifestation of the Heptapods' vision of the world is the meaning that Fermat's principle takes on when applied to light refraction. This principle states that a ray of light will travel from point A to point C via whatever trajectory will minimize the time traveled. Of course, in a homogenous medium, such as air, this path will be a straight line from A to C. However, if the observation point C is, for instance, in water, the ray will travel from A to C via the point B, situated on the surface of the water, according to the following figure:

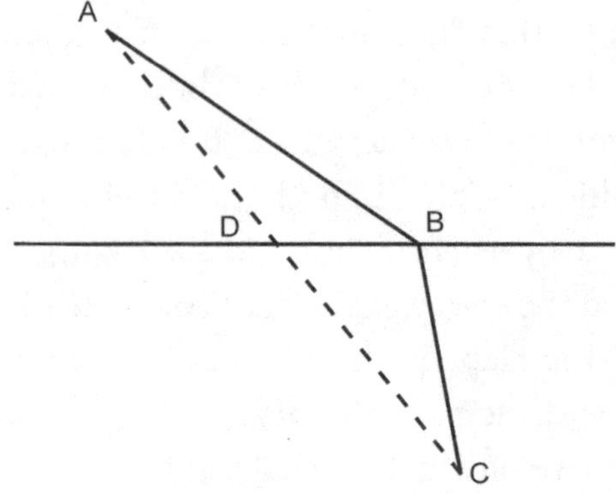

Given that the mediums of air and water are characterized by different refractive indexes, the ray of light will travel faster in the first than in the second. If it follows the straight line AC, the time it spends between the point D where it meets the surface of the water and the destination of point C will be such that it would be faster to first travel to B in order to pass through water on the path BC, which is shorter than the path DC. In this case, the straight line is indeed the shortest path from point A to point C, but it is not the fastest.

We may notice that the language used to explain Fermat's principle seems to give the ray of light an intention, a goal according to which it calculates and chooses the path that will minimize the time traveled. Fermat's theorem was criticized for this way of looking at things, which seems to substitute a certain teleology for the scientific mechanism of cause and effect. It is this finalistic language, as it happens, that resonates with the Heptapods, who, on the other hand, prove, curiously, to be uninterested when the physicist tries to ask them about algebra and other sciences. This interest leads the linguist in Chiang's novella to wonder, "What kind of worldview did the Heptapods have, that they would consider Fermat's Principle the simplest explanation of light refraction? What kind of perception made a minimum or maximum readily apparent to them?"[29] For them, as we may recall, the end was in the beginning; "premises and conclusions were interchangeable."[30]

A crucial aspect of the philosophical fiction Chiang imagines is that the Heptapod language branches into Heptapod A and Heptapod B, which are their oral and written languages, respectively. A distinctive characteristic of the extraterrestrials, which the linguist discovers upon inviting her otherworldly interlocutors to switch to writing so that they can teach her their language, is that, in fact, their writing is not simply the transcription of their speech. Heptapod A and Heptapod B fulfill radically different cognitive functions; while in speech, phonemes necessarily must come one after the other in a linear succession in time, in writing, graphemes coexist in the same space and time, where they are stuck together in a "conglomeration," to use the linguist's word.

Of course, we are within a philosophical "fiction," but we should note that the idea of a written language entirely different from speech would rule in favor of Jacques Derrida in his opposition to phonocentrism, according to which speech is the primary, unadulterated presence of meaning, which makes it, for this reason, superior to writing, which is merely the transcription thereof. The language Heptapod B is in fact reversible; it can be read from front to back and/or from back to front, in the same way as the Heptapods walk—since they have eyes all around their bodies, they move neither forward nor backward. Within its nonlinear orthography it carries a vision of reality in which one begins with effects in order to create, through action, the causes.

By deciphering their language, Louise Banks learns to enter into their vision. Consequently, the pages of the *Book of Ages* will be opened for her. This is the name by which Chiang imagines a "Borgesian" text, as he calls it, in which everything, past, present, and future, is recorded. In this book, the linguist will have before her very eyes *the story of your life*, which she tells, in the second person, to her daughter, Hannah—an obvious palindrome—whose death she will live in her birth, whose end will be her beginning.

In Chiang's novella, a particular emphasis is placed on the theme of predestination and the wisdom that lies in being able to embrace destiny, that of humanity as well as one's own, when one knows it, without wanting to change a thing. At the end, when the Heptapods abruptly leave in the same way as they came, after a gift-giving ceremony, we understand that the real gift they gave their hosts is this superior wisdom to which the Heptapod language and their knowledge of the future gives access. Their official present, superconducting materials whose secrets they teach humans, is ultimately without interest, as it has already been discovered in Japan. The secret lies elsewhere: what they offer to Louise, for her to transmit, is the key to a new world.

This very secret is, of course, likewise revealed in the translation from the book to the movie, but *Arrival*'s ultimate message is different: the higher wisdom that the film brings to the forefront, and which the Heptapods give to humanity, goes beyond the mere capacity to gain access to another way of perceiving reality. What these visitors from beyond the stars give to humanity is humanity itself. It is the ethics of translation that consists in *achieving humanity together.*

The individuals settled in the twelve places chosen by the extraterrestrials in order to communicate with humans start by collaborating and sharing the information they collect on the language and likely intentions of their visitors. But rather quickly their ulterior motives are to be cast in broad daylight and end up blowing up, in a literal as well as a figurative sense (in a literal sense when, in Montana, a group of American soldiers, unbeknownst to their superiors, take the initiative to set off a bomb in two of the Heptapods' spaceships, mortally wounding one of them), the collaboration with the aliens on one hand, and among the different countries where they landed on the other.

When the visitors use a word whose translation they are unsure of, hesitating between "weapon" and "tool," China decides that these "others" must be enemies, and it is only at the last minute that Louise Banks persuades their leader not to attack the Heptapods' spaceship.

This belligerent explosion is the effect of the tribal instinct in spite of which, as Henri Bergson wrote, we have to acquire a sense of humanity through philosophical reasoning and religion.[31] We can clearly understand the symbolism of the number 12, which Chiang chose in reference to the biblical twelve tribes of Israel, and more precisely, in the Epistle of James, "to the twelve tribes in the dispersion." The Heptapods will ultimately make way once again for the stars, but not before leaving two messages for the Earthlings. The first takes the form of a puzzle, divided into twelve pieces addressed to each of the twelve tribes. In order to translate it and reap the benefits of its content, they will have to collaborate, to achieve humanity together. The second is that, if they gave their hosts the gift of the worldview carried by their language, it is because in three thousand years they will have need of the new humanity created by this encounter of the third kind.

There is give and take, even regarding a promise for a distant future. But what does time even signify from this point forward? What counts most of all lies in the meaning of this exchange, which is not a transaction but charity. In this regard, a critical scene in the book and the film comes when Hannah asks her mom, the linguist, the word for an exchange in which each party wins. Over "win-win," which her mother suggests, she declares that she prefers a more scholarly term. "Non-zero-sum game" will ultimately be the expression she retains. Indeed, such is the nature of the game the extraterrestrials, like their interlocutors, through translation, through an exchange from language to language, have all won, when they achieve humanity together.

At the end of the day, whether it's the anthropological thought experiment or the fiction of radical translation, the lesson is the same. No matter the distance that separates them, translation puts in touch and *compares* languages. We shall now put this lesson to the test of colonial domination.

# 2.

# THE *TRUCHEMENT* AND THE TRANSLATOR

♦

I would say that just as there are pirate radios, there is a pirate usage of language, and that this is what a minor literature is. Yes, in a sense, Negro literature of French expression is also a pirate literature. Of course it is not exhausted by such a definition. Specifically, we must not content ourselves with the observation that a language has been abducted and hijacked. We must go to the trouble of studying what the language has become in the hands of those who took hold of it and whether, in the end, we are talking about the same tongue. Or at the very least, the same language.

A language hijacked, most likely.

A language corrupted, assuredly.

But perhaps a language reloaded as well, and dynamized.[1]

—AIMÉ CÉSAIRE

AMADOU HAMPÂTÉ BÂ (1901–1991) presents a scene of translation in the biography he devoted to the man who was his teacher, master, and spiritual guide in Mali during the period of French colonial rule, where he was born: Tierno Bokar Salif Tall, otherwise known as "the sage of Bandiagara."[2] The scene opens on the latter's court appearance before the representative of the colonial administration in the Malian town of Mopti, to answer for the crime of being anti-French, since he had been affiliated with a religious movement reputed to be opposed to France's action in its West African colonies. The movement in question, of the so-called eleven beads, as its members had the custom of reciting a particular prayer eleven times, was a dissident branch of a Sufi brotherhood, the Tijaniyya, whose politics generally sought to accommodate the colonial power. The majority of the disciples in this mystic order had adopted the practice of reciting the prayer in question twelve times, not eleven. Between the "twelves" and the "elevens," the rift had become profound; it even separated members of the Tall family, recognized as the primary leaders of the Tijaniyya in West Africa. Tierno himself likewise came from this family, but, with his "eleven" prayer beads, he was part of the minority considered to be dissident and rebellious by the majority of the Tall clan, which for the colonial administration constituted an "establishment" and an ally.

## THE *TRUCHEMENT*'S CUNNING

It came to be that the commander of the Mopti Circle,[3] by the name of Levavasseur, summoned Tierno to decide whether, after a hearing, he should be let free or imprisoned.

We must remember that the colonial administrator effectively had total power, including judicial authority, over the natives. With the man fulfilling the role of interpreter at his side, allowing him to understand these subjects of France, and allowing these subjects to understand the orders and decisions he wished to transmit to them, Levavasseur received Tierno accompanied by several notable figures, including one of his parents of the Tall clan, for an appearance upon which his freedom depended.

Feeling ill-tempered and eager to get things over with, the administrator went right to the point: "Tierno Bokar," he asked, in French, naturally, "are you prepared to return to the practice of which you are one of the great leaders (that is, of the 'twelve beads') and for all to be said and done, yes or no?"[4] The interpreter, by the name of Oumar Sy, who was meant to transmit the commander's question into Tierno's language, subsequently delivered the following "translation": "Tijani Aguibou Tall, the chief of Bandiagara, along with notable guests, has come here so that you may return with him to Bandiagara. Are you prepared to follow him?"

To which the master obviously replied with a "yes," accompanied by an eloquent nod of the head that Levavasseur did not need to have translated. Oumar Sy, the interpreter, thus took it upon himself to follow this with a comment to the commander indicating that Tierno could never disobey his elder coming to ask him to follow him, to return to the great Tall family and to readopt the spiritual practice of the twelve beads with which it had always been associated. Tierno thus left, free, and the commander Levavasseur, satisfied to see order reestablished, was finally able to conclude in his report to the circle's *Register-Journal*: "Today, Tierno Bokar Salif Tall and members of his family presented themselves to me. The marabout Tierno Bokar is readopting the 'twelve beads' and abandoning the practice of 'eleven beads.' His people came to retrieve him. All is settled. The matter is resolved."[5]

Here it is undoubtedly necessary, in a long parenthetical, to explain in greater depth the "matter" at hand; to explain the Tijaniyya and the Picrocholine[6] warlike opposition between the eleven beads and the twelve beads.

Bokar Salif Tall, respectfully referred to as "Tierno," or "master" in the Fulani language, was a spiritual guide in the mystic order called Tijaniyya, named for its founder, the sheikh Ahmad al-Tidjani. The latter, born in Aïn Madhi in Algeria, had lived and taught the philosophy and practices of his branch of Sufism in Fes, in Morocco, where he died and was buried in 1815. Among the prayers that were regularly recited by the disciples of this order while keeping track with their prayer beads, there is one regarding the prophet of Islam called "The Jewel of Perfection," which the texts of this branch say must be recited eleven times, while counting the eleven beads. As the tradition goes, it was one day recited twelve times, when the founder of the Tijaniyya himself was only able to join his disciples by the time they had already finished the psalmody. They therefore added an additional recitation so that their master could say "The Jewel of Perfection" with them. This practice thereby established the tradition of the twelve beads alongside the eleven, giving the latter a claim to textual orthodoxy.

Though it was born in North Africa, it was farther south, from Senegal to Sudan, that the Tijani branch had the most disciples. The order spread throughout West Africa in particular, on one hand through the "jihad," which was driven by one of the main leaders of the branch, the sheikh El Hadj Omar Tall, who died in Bandiagara, Mali, in 1864, but on the other hand and more importantly through missionary action by local spiritual guides. The members of the Tall family took their prestige from their ancestor El Hadj Omar. It was during the 1920s that there developed, in the region formed by the territories of Mali, Mauritania, and Senegal, a Tijani branch practicing the eleven beads whose spiritual leader was the sheikh Hamallah. When they found themselves at odds with the colonial administration, the dispute that constituted their opposition to the twelve-bead majority took an extremely violent turn in a political direction. The sheikh Hamallah was subsequently imprisoned from 1925 to 1930, then exiled for five more years in Ivory Coast. Freed in 1936 upon the Front Populaire's coming to power, he returned to his city, Nioro, in Mali. Still considered to be "anti-French," he was suspected of preparing an anticolonial jihad. He was eventually arrested again in 1940 and deported to France in 1942, where he would die the following year. He was buried in Montluçon.

Tierno Bokar adopted the practice of the eleven beads in 1937, the year when he met the sheikh Hamallah, in a "conversion" that the majority of the Tall family viewed as a betrayal. Shortly after the scene that has just been described, it was discovered that the matter was not resolved, as Levavasseur had believed it to be, and that Tierno had never renounced the practice of the eleven beads. This pacifist whose life and teachings have often evoked comparisons to Saint Francis of Assisi thus came to face banishment and house arrest until his death in 1940 put an end to his persecution. Oumar Sy, Governor Levavasseur's interpreter, had only delayed what would eventually come to pass. But Tierno Bokar's calvary only added to his saintlike reputation.

What the judgment scene and interpreter's ruse show us is, first of all, that colonization needs translators. When one intends not to meet the other in their language but rather to subject them to his, one is confronted by the necessity expressed by the historian and British politician Lord Thomas Macaulay (1800–1859) in his famous "Minute" of 1835 on "Indian Education" and the best way to spend the funds allocated toward the "intellectual improvement of the people of this country."[7]

Making what was, for him, the straightforward observation that "the dialects commonly spoken among the natives of... India contain neither literary nor scientific information," Macaulay affirms that immense enrichment would be necessary were one to "translate any valuable work into them." They could therefore only be nurtured by a language distinct from all these vernacular ways of speaking. Macaulay wondered if that language could be Arabic or Sanskrit, that is to say, the languages of the "Hindoo" and "Mahometan" laws; in a way, the recognition they receive here could be understood as evidence of a certain openness and willingness to cooperate on the part of the British power.

But this question was purely rhetorical, and he wasted no time setting it aside. One could not seriously consider choosing such languages that had not, even in their poetry, produced anything even slightly comparable to the output of the languages of "great European nations"! As for "cooperation," why would the people whose role it was to learn have anything to say about the language of their education, when such a decision was the exclusive privilege of the schoolmasters?

Thus English was to be the language of the education and intellectual development of the natives, since, Macaulay notes, "it stands preeminent even among the languages of the West." It would be for India what Greek and Latin were for Europe, the British lord added, concluding that, given the constraints that limited resources impose,

> We must at present do our best to form a class who may be interpreters between us and the millions whom we govern; a class of persons Indian in blood and colour, but English in tastes, in opinions, in morals, and in intellect. To that class we may leave it to refine the vernacular dialects of the country, to enrich those dialects with terms of science borrowed from the Western nomenclature, and to render them by degrees fit vehicles for conveying knowledge to the great mass of the population.[8]

Interpreters, then, are needed for colonization and administration. But they must be nothing more than that, mere "vehicles," as Macaulay says. In other words, mere "*truchements*." We should note that in French, while this word, borrowed from the Arabic *tarjumān*, meaning "translator," does in fact conserve this original meaning, it is now most commonly used only to mean "instrument" or "means." The colonial interpreter is required to be a *truchement*, an intermediary by way of whom the imperial word is to be conveyed to "the millions whom we govern," and who, conversely, will pass upward any information needed by the decision makers. The role of Oumar Sy, in the mind of Commander Levavasseur, was only to be such a "*truchement*."

Here, however, he has come to assume the role of mediator. Therein lies the second lesson implicit in the judgment scene of Tierno Bokar before the commander: the colonial administration cannot prevent those occupying the special position of intermediary from also becoming mediators.[9]

Indeed, what did Oumar Sy accomplish by manipulating his superior?

Levavasseur asked a closed question that called unambiguously for a yes or no answer, and he could therefore presume that Oumar Sy would simply be the channel through which his words in French would be transformed into words in Fulani, without any of the crystal-clear meaning of his question getting lost in translation. And, in the other direction, he could count on the fact that the accused's response would come back to him salva veritate in the imperial language, along with, moreover, physical signs, body language, indicating a positive or negative answer whose meaning one could believe to be universal.

But here the interpreter has made himself into an agent, no longer a mere instrument. He has manifested the reality of what Homi Bhabha referred to as a "third space"[10] within the colonial empire, simultaneously taking part in the imperium and the world of the colonized. This space, which now draws the attention of historians of colonization and specialists in translation studies alike, is that of auxiliary agents of the administration, and particularly interpreters, who redefined their role as one that goes beyond being a mere *truchement* in order to become veritable *cultural mediators.*

Oumar Sy, then, is a mediator. Whereas Levavasseur expects a simple situation calling for a unilinear interaction from which a decision would automatically emerge, Oumar Sy knows that to translate is to take into account the totality of the cultural context in all its complexity and that it can never be the purely technical transposition of words from one language into another.

For Levavasseur, the matter was as linear as a sequence of equations: *eleven beads = anti-France = bedlam = not in my house.* All the while, for his interpreter, it was necessary to understand the totality of the situation, which is hardly possible by way of a closed question to which one is meant to respond "yes" or "no." Since, yes, Tierno has indeed become a member of the sect of eleven beads. And no, he is not a troublemaker, but rather a man of study, teaching, and contemplation, who went from twelve beads to eleven, not motivated by an opposition to France but for purely spiritual reasons. Oumar Sy's manipulative interpreting was not, in this sense, an act of betrayal or of treason, but rather, a veritable act of translation, as it properly reflected the situation in its totality. From this point of view, it was, even, truly sincere.

We shall say, in a word, that the interpreter made himself, out of the *truchement* that he was, into a translator. That is to suggest that a translator is someone who has a complete cultural understanding of a situation, and that this is what is imparted, rather than a mere conveyance or transferal from one language to another. It is therefore unsurprising that those whom the French colonial administration in Africa recruited to be *truchements* would quite often become writers who translated into the imperial language the orature[11] of their cultures.

## TRANSLATING ORATURE

In this way, Amadou Hampâté Bâ, for one, to whom we are indebted for the account of the life and teachings of his master Tierno Bokar, and who is one of the most famous translators of orature into francophone literature, began his career as an interpreter for the colonial administration. Like many others, he quickly transformed his position of *writer-interpreter*, which was the official title for this type of ancillary, into that of simply *writer*: ceasing to be "the voice of his master," the *truchement* has now found his own. The interpreter has become an interpreter of himself[12] and of his culture, that is to say, a *translator*.

Amadou Hampâté Bâ is famous, among other things, for championing the preservation of treasures of orature from the perils of forgetfulness and loss. Since orature is a literature (which should be understood simultaneously as knowledge and humanity) written in the living memory of those who transmit it, he made the following declaration, which has now become a proverb: "An elder who dies is a library in flames." The only way to save this library is to tear it out of its container, living today but betrothed to death, in order to give its hand to the perennity of writing. We must, then, *trans-vase* memory.[13]

Some will emphasize the contradictory character of preserving living speech in writing, which we should recall, and as Plato may remind us, is its very petrification. They might also add that the death of orature is twofold: first when it becomes writing and second when it is transferred into the colonial language, becoming literature. They take the notion of African literature of French *expression*, for example, as a capitulation and an oxymoron.

A capitulation, since bringing orature into existence in the colonial language is to surrender and to pay a tribute to it. In Pascale Casanova's terms, to translate into French is to acknowledge its "hypercentrality" and superiority, and thus to admit that orature needs to be *uplifted* to exist in French. An oxymoron because when expressed in French, the African imagination would lose its soul, that is, its Africanness.

In contrast to this understanding of linguistic nationalism, according to which literature can be African only if it is written in an *African language*, we shall maintain that literature, which I would call a *literature of translation*, has precisely made English, French, and Portuguese into *languages of Africa*. We shall call a literature of translation that which has developed within the genre of "folktale" in Africa under French colonization, and within which such authors as Amadou Hampâté Bâ, Bernard Dadié of Ivory Coast (1916–2019), Birago Diop of Senegal (1906–1989), and even Léopold Sédar Senghor (1906–2001) have distinguished themselves. We must not forget, in fact, that Senghor was likewise, along with Abdoulaye Sadji (1910–1961), the co-author of a children's book, which is a translation into French, entitled *La Belle histoire de Leuk-le-Lièvre* [The great story of Leuk the Hare], of the adventures of this animal, hero of numerous stories from the countries of the West African savanna.[14]

This reader for primary school students is made up of a series of folktales translated from orature in which the main character is the hare—*leuk* in Wolof—who is cunning incarnate. These stories are organized in such a way as to form an actual narrative, from the moment when Leuk himself announces his own birth to the moment when he finishes educating the son of Man, brother of Lion, king of the jungle, preparing him for the responsibility of ruling with the wisdom he acquired growing up among the animals, employing it in that other type of jungle that is the world of humans. Senghor and Sadji arrange these stories from orature according to an arc that makes them into a more or less continuous narrative and a true bildungsroman.

Such is an example of what it can mean to re-create orature in literature, with all the faithfulness and requisite betrayal that constitute the task of the translator. The same could be said of the collection put together by Bernard Dadié entitled *Le Pagne noir*,[15] or *Contes d'Amadou Koumba* as well as *Les Nouveaux Contes d'Amadou Koumba*, by Birago Diop.[16]

Before returning to this writer and his reconstitution in French of the stories he gathered from Amadou Koumba, it must be acknowledged that the history of this genre seems, at first glance, to rule in favor of those who see within a literature of translation a tribute paid to the imperial language.

Oftentimes, its authors were in fact colonial administrators publishing "translations" that represented, generally speaking, the epitome of what Antoine Berman would call "appropriative and reductive." Let us add: condescending. These administrators, to whom, it must be said, we are indebted for many early collections of oral texts, had, as Ralph Austen writes, "concerned themselves professionally with the control of Africans and thus viewed the study of indigenous literature as a valuable key to 'native psychology.'"[17] We have one such example in the book published in 1913 by François-Victor Équilbecq, deputy administrator of the colonies of his state, entitled *Essai sur la littérature merveilleuse des Noirs suivi de Contes indigènes de l'Ouest africain français* [Essay on the marvelous Black literature, followed by Native Tales of French West Africa].[18] And it is entirely as an "appropriative" translation, as a translation tool, that the preface written by Maurice Delafosse, who signs it as "Head Colonial Administrator," presents the work:

> To properly know a race of humans, to assess their mentality, to unearth their processes of reasoning, and to comprehend their moral and intellectual life, there is nothing quite like studying their folklore, that is to say, a naive, unfussy literature, straight from the soul of the people, delivering it to us in all its primitive nakedness.[19]

For his part, Austen notes that missionaries likewise acted as translators of numerous oral texts:

> Because of the commitment of missionaries to particular regions of Africa and their need to learn local languages for purposes of evangelization (and especially Bible translation), the conditions under which they produced oral literature texts often come closer to the ideals of contemporary scholars than do those of administrators. We thus have bilingual texts (or even texts exclusively in local languages).[20]

The distinction between translations by administrators and those by missionaries is significant. The latter translate in two directions: the Bible into indigenous languages, and indigenous orature into imperial European languages. At the very heart of their work of translating, they encounter the mutual hospitality that two languages, able to coexist from that moment on, can offer each other.

The Gambian and American theologian Lamin Sanneh (1942–2019) dedicated a remarkable book[21] to developing our understanding of the meaning of translation for "the mission," calling into question the common preconception according to which it was wholly in line with the so-called civilizing mission of colonization. This meaning, he points out, should be understood on the contrary as a form of respect for African languages and cultures insofar as they can and should become repositories for the *Message*.

That may well be. However, even as missionaries reject the "reductive" and condescending conception of translation, they nevertheless share with the administrators, largely speaking, the act of carrying out its "appropriative" function. This can be seen, for example, in the frequently made selection of oral texts that take the form of cosmogonic myths that demonstrate, in translation, their compatibility with monotheism and the biblical account of creation.[22] It is likewise toward this sort of flattening of the texts into a purely documentary function that the ethnographers' translations most often proceeded, even if they were pursuing different ends.

Literature of translation, by such authors as Bernard Dadié and Birago Diop, is not the continuation of this "genre" marked by its colonial origins. It is, on the contrary, the deconstruction thereof. These authors turned the translation of orature into something entirely different from what imperial appropriation had constructed under the label "folklore." They shaped it into a *literature* created by reciprocal hospitality between languages which they *put in touch*, enacting what is for Antoine Berman the essence of translation.

It is not simply because they were Africans and that their work represented a sort of indigenization of translation. It is because they knew how to decenter the imperial language, how to impose upon it the sweet violence of mixing created by the trade from language to language.[23]

For that matter, they had in a certain sense a predecessor in Blaise Cendrars (1887–1961), poet and author in 1921 of *Anthologie nègre* [Negro anthology], which broke with translations that had been put forth up to that point. Granted, Cendrars merely compiled the "folktales" collected and translated by colonial administrators, missionaries, and anthropologists: his anthology repeated, in large part, the work of François-Victor Équilbecq. And of course, as writes Christine Le Quellec Cottier, he failed to "distance himself from the then dominant colonialist and evolutionist ideology."[24]

The fact remains that his entire enterprise is contrary to a condescending and *appropriative* translation. For him, transferal into the imperial language is not a valorization of orature by the "hypercenter"; it is, on the contrary, a loss of being, as the brief "notice" states, which he writes in order to introduce the anthology rather than a preface or introduction, which would have dictated the manner in which the composite texts should be read: he considers that "objects and tales demand to be discovered for themselves, in and of themselves, without any analytical intermediary."[25]

In his "notice," after mentioning the "linguistic research" that demonstrates, according to him, that "nobody in Europe can henceforth deny that Black Africa is one of the most linguistically rich lands there is," Cendrars indicates that this research "unanimously praises the beauty and plastic power of these languages" and that "there are perhaps no other languages in the world with more defined a character and more precision in their expression."[26] There is, evidently, within these words and these dithyrambic accolades a certain will to persuade, but two points are significant in the "notice": the emphasis placed on the *languages* of the folktales, and the insistence upon their literariness. These texts are not expected to open up the indigenous soul but to express their literature, to show how they play with their own words.

Cendrars refers to certain stories as modern, and he erases any references and elements that would flatten them into being essentially documentary or "ethnographic" in value. His goal is to restore "their living source and... thereby recreate them."[27] The collection of these stories such that they "form an artistic rather than ethnographic entity"[28] is what made the publication of *Anthologie nègre* the literary event that it was. Offering, in print, a joyful relationship to language and narrative: this likewise led Cendrars to draw from his *Anthologie*, several years later, children's stories.

And, regarding the African languages from which these stories were translated, the poet incites us to imagine what "beauty" and "plastic power" they must possess such that, once welcomed into a European language, the imagination that they bear is able to hold on to, despite what is *lost* in translation, the greatest possible life force. It is up to us, then, to imagine the source language as possessing even more *being* than what is evidenced by its transcription into a European idiom.

The notion of something lost in translation into French and, simultaneously, a sense of jubilation for these languages being thus put in touch and mixed is precisely what is expressed by the reinvention of the genre of "folklore" by the *truchement*, turned writer, who was Amadou Hampâté Bâ, but also by such quintessential writers of this genre as Bernard Dadié and Birago Diop.

## A LANGUAGE INSEMINATED

Birago Diop, in fact, was fond of saying, with regards to his inventive reworking of oral texts, that he was a mere translator, that is, a pallid impersonator of the oral performances of the griot Amadou Koumba, which were much better and much livelier. Giving his two collections the titles *Les Contes d'Amadou Koumba* and *Les Nouveaux Contes d'Amadou Koumba* (Tales of Amadou Koumba and New Tales of Amadou Koumba) allowed him to place on the covers of the books the name of the true author in Wolof, the "living source" of the texts, Amadou Koumba, alongside his own, that of the translator into French.

Indeed, it is critical for Birago Diop to call himself a "translator" of the griot in order to signify that orature is already literature, as a performance in a precise language, with its own narrative techniques, and not the manifestation of some collective "spirit," waiting to be given form, meaning, and value in and by the hypercentral language.

Léopold Sédar Senghor wrote the preface to *Les Nouveaux Contes d'Amadou Koumba*, in which he responds to what, eleven years earlier, had been Birago Diop's own introduction to his first collection of Koumba's folktales. The latter writes,

> If I was unable to bring to what I tell here the atmosphere in which I basked as a listener, like those that I saw around me, attentive, trembling, meditative, it is because I have become a man, that is, an unfinished child, and am hence incapable of re-creating the marvelous. Above all, I lack the voice, the flair, and the mimicry of my dear old griot. On the solid loom of his stories and sentences, using his smooth heddle, I had hoped, shoddy weaver that I am, hesitating here and there, to fashion a few strips to stitch together a cloth in which Grandmother, if she were to return, would find the cotton that she first had spun; and in which Amadou Koumba would recognize the coloring, now much less vibrant, of the beautiful fabrics that he had woven for me all those years ago.[29]

Senghor's preface responds to this comparison of the translated text to a woven cloth having lost the vibrancy of its original colors in the operation when he declares that we should make no mistake when Diop calls himself solely the griot's *traduttore* and thus inevitably his *traditore*. This should be seen merely as "modesty," if not coyness, on the part of the author.[30]

It is Birago Diop, in reality, who re-creates these stories, which take on a different life, one that is full, strong, and new in a language that is no longer foreign from the moment that it embraces the orature to which the translator has opened it, in which the language of performance does not disappear but continues to exist and to produce literary effects.

In "Orphée Noir," the preface he wrote for Senghor's *Anthologie de la nouvelle poésie nègre et malgache de langue française*,[31] Jean-Paul Sartre read in the writing of the Black poets there assembled a way for the indigenous of the empire to appropriate the colonial language for themselves, to turn it inside out so as to express another ontology, another aesthetic, a truth other than the imperial truths. Sartre's text remains one of the best definitions of what it means to *write back*: to carry out a decentering of the hypercentral language to engage it in its becoming-African.

More specifically, the philosopher points out that in no one else's writing more so than that of Birago Diop can we feel, in the purest classical French, as written by this poet who was above all a storyteller, the presence of an African orature and language. And it is this writing of a dual presence of languages that makes the characteristic style of Birago Diop and, more broadly, of an African literature in French: a style of the in-between, an aesthetic of the language-to-language.

When he reflects upon the ambivalence of the translator, who "wants to force from both sides": "to force his own language to adorn itself with strangeness, and to force the other language to trans-port itself into his mother tongue," Antoine Berman naturally turns, in a lengthy endnote, to the position of "non-French writers writing in French" and to "literatures of francophone countries."[32] Their "foreign French," as he calls it, their manner of "inhabiting our language," is the greatest illustration of what he calls translation: that its essence is a cross-fertilization. The Mauritian poet Édouard Maunick, whom Berman cites at the end of the note, put it well: it is a matter of "inseminating French."

# 3.

# TRANSLATIONS OF CLASSICAL AFRICAN ART

◆

> Now more than ever, objects are migratory, and among them, men, cultures, and languages. What would happen if we truly realized this, as a fact demarcating this era, different from ancient human migrations and all sorts of colonialisms? How would we define this new age of translational transfer in which we are currently living?[1]
>
> —BARBARA CASSIN AND DANIÈLE WOZNY

ON NOVEMBER 28, 2017, at the University of Ouagadougou, in Burkina Faso, French president Emmanuel Macron delivered an address expressing his will to rebuild relations between his country and Africa on new grounds. As a sign thereof, he recognized that, since a considerable amount of classical African art was found primarily in the museums of Europe, there was a dispossession that demanded reparation. "African heritage," he then said, "cannot solely exist in private collections and European museums. African heritage must be showcased in Paris but also in Dakar, Lagos, and Cotonou; this will be one of my priorities."

Felwine Sarr and Bénédicte Savoy were then asked to prepare a report on the methods of what was announced in the address as "temporary or definitive returns of African heritage to Africa." The authors wasted no time in doing so, and their report became an important reflection not only on the potential process of restitution but also on the role it could play in defining future relations between museums of the Global North and Global South.[2]

The address at Ouagadougou thus set in motion a dynamic that has already led to the restitution of certain objects to Benin and Senegal, but "Africa's struggle to see its heritage returned" has a long history that began well before the birth of President Macron. The expression "Africa's struggle for its art" is also the title of the work Bénédicte Savoy published following the report she co-authored, in order to clarify the different stages that mark the long road toward "the return of an irreplaceable cultural heritage to those who created it," in the words of Amadou-Mahtar M'Bow, cited in the Sarr-Savoy report.[3]

Indeed, among the various significant dates that serve as milestones of this long struggle, Savoy singles out 1978, the year of the ever-famous speech by M'Bow, then director-general of UNESCO. The following excerpt was the core of this speech, in which he speaks of the peoples who, along with their artistic heritage, "have been dispossessed" of a certain "memory":

> [These peoples] know, of course, that art is for the world and are aware of the fact that this art, which tells the story of their past and shows what they really are, does not speak

> to them alone. They are happy that men and women elsewhere can study and admire the work of their ancestors. They also realize that certain works of art have for too long played too intimate a part in the history of the country to which they were taken for the symbols linking them with that country to be denied, and for the roots they have put down to be severed.[4]

We should make note of the inscription of works of art into two different metaphoric registers that would have them be plants on one hand, language on the other.

## THE FORCE OF FETISHES

To thus compare African objects to sorts of rhizomes that always put down roots in "the country to which they were taken" is to remember that their voyage is not a mere displacement but also, literally, a *transplantation*. To say that these objects "speak," that they "tell" a "story," their "truth" in their original language, but that they are also open to the language of "men and women elsewhere" in "the country to which they were taken," away from the lands where they were created, is to say that their voyage is also a *translation*.[5]

To employ the concepts of *transplantation* and *translation* is not to forget that, in many cases, colonial violence is at the origin of the transfer of works of art into ethnographic museums in Europe, where they were long held as "curiosities," or even as ethnographic "monstrosities": "fetishes," as they were called. Rather, these concepts insist upon the fact that African objects have not stayed inert in these museums but have proved to be forces of life and transformation, that their vivacity carries on, as the vegetal metaphor indicates. And the concept of translation tells us that this vivacity means they have found life in new languages, thus becoming *mediators* and making their translators mediators as well.

These translator-mediators were those who were designated as "primitivists," to use a word that Philippe Dagen notes has remained "in use," as likewise evidenced by the title, *Primitivism*, under which the Museum of Modern Art in New York City, the MoMA, organized a wave-making exhibition in 1984.[6] The concept of primitivism has a history that Dagen relates as follows:

> At the beginning of the twentieth century, young artists, first in Germany and France, took sudden interest in objects coming primarily from Oceania in Germany and from Africa in France. These artists were the founders of the avant-garde movements called Die Brücke in Dresden, fauvism and cubism in Paris, and, soon after, Der Blaue Reiter in Munich. Their names are the best known of their time: Henri Matisse, André Derain, Pablo Picasso, Georges Braque, Ernst Ludwig Kirchner, Emil Nolde, Max Pechstein, Paul Klee, Vassily Kandinsky, Franz Marc. They were preceded by Paul Gauguin, whose travels and works are well renowned. Because of them, artifacts that had been until then relegated to ethnographic museums or circulated via hazardous channels of flea markets ceased to be little more than monstrous and grotesque monstrosities, and thus gained access to the status of artwork, capable of exerting influence over their discoverers and admirers. After the First World War, this process, broadening and gaining a wider audience, began

anew with the Dada movement and surrealism, with André Breton, Paul Éluard, Jean Arp, Joan Miró, Alberto Giacometti, and André Masson. Such is a summary description of the plot and its main protagonists.[7]

The word *primitivist* suggests that it was the European avant-gardes who created African arts. They turned speechless artifacts into works of art, and lent absolutely *absurd* objects a comprehensible language. These are fetishes-turned-art, but *primitive* art. In actuality, the sudden interest of which they were the object is that which is born of the sort of nostalgia one may feel for a state before civilization, for a primal condition of man not yet corrupted by progress and modernity. A certain comparative approach founded on the principle that societies and humans that share such a condition display the same characteristics would establish that the populations of regions as distant as New Guinea, Gabon, or the Marquesas Islands, but likewise the deranged or the populations of Europe untouched by progress, will quite naturally create analogous artifacts reflective of the same primal state; this state is likewise that of children.[8] Primitivism is a Eurocentric and lazy concept.

Its Eurocentrism would hold that these *primitive* artifacts themselves ultimately had nothing to do with the transmutation they underwent into pieces of art, nor a fortiori with the direction in which they steered modern artistic creation. At best they were intermediaries, *truchements*, by way of which the avant-gardes were able to reconnect with a primal state that had been buried beneath "progress." Thus the avant-gardes were the sole inventors of what, at the beginning of the twentieth century, was called "Negro art."

The concept likewise is lazy, as it authorizes an adherence to apparent morphological resemblances, without care or sensitivity to differences. There isn't the slightest need to accurately examine masks and sculptures in order to move toward the "philosophies" of which they are the visual language. It suffices to invoke some vague capacity for inspiring avant-garde Europeans among the general features of the art said to be "primitive."

Therefore, African arts seen through primitivism are not the actual objects identified for their impact on the course of artistic modernism, but rather solely the imagination of European poets and artists creating new visual languages, drawing on their own inner resources while simultaneously constructing meanings to assign to "primitive" creations. This way of reading their arts indiscriminately "reflects," as Joshua Cohen writes, "the ideational quagmire of what literary critic Christopher Miller has called 'blank darkness,' wherein Africa functions as a screen for the projection of Western fantasies and epistemologies."[9]

Against these "efforts to minimize, erase, or negate the roles played by African and other non-Western visual traditions in modernism's development,"[10] art historians such as Philippe Dagen and Joshua Cohen have now called primitivism into question, along with its "stubborn narrative of the European self-sufficient genius."[11]

Consequently, against this "ideational quagmire," we must conduct an accurate examination, a close reading of the *translations* erstwhile carried out by European artists, in the position of mediators, of the visual language of artifacts that were themselves mediators as well, not intermediaries or *truchements*, mere points of reference to inspire artists who would eventually dismiss them, saying, decidedly, "Negro art? Never heard of it!" In this way, an important aspect of Joshua Cohen's work consists in following the trace of certain identified sculptures all the way to their translation into the language of specific modern works. Maurice de Vlaminck, for instance, recounts having acquired, one afternoon in the year 1905, in a bar in Argenteuil, three statuettes that revealed to him, he tells us, "Negro art" and stirred the furthest reaches of his being that day, according to his own words. This drove him to purchase a whole ensemble of African sculptures from a friend of his father, who was trying to get rid of them. Among these was a "white Fang mask," which he hung above his bed before eventually passing it to his friend André Derain, who insisted on having it. It was in the latter's studio that the mask was seen by Picasso and Matisse, who were utterly stupefied by it.[12]

To call this one of the points when "Negro art" began to be in vogue is insufficient. It is important to follow the trajectory of the Fang mask to the moment it finds its translation in Vlaminck's *Les Baigneuses* and Derain's *La Danse*, just as a Kru mask from Ivory Coast would find its translation in 1912 in Picasso's guitar series.[13]

Moreover, as concerns translation and mediation, we may recall that Picasso used the word *intercession*, highlighting its significance, in a dialogue reconstructed by Malraux: the artist ventures that African masks, far from being "sculptures like any others," were "intercessors," adding that it was from that moment on that he knew this word in French.[14] This is ultimately what Amadou-Mahtar M'Bow said regarding works that are symbolically linked to "the country to which they were taken." In the starkest contrast to the domination that the label *primitivism*[15] carries within itself, intercession creates, in the spirit of reciprocity, a symbolic relationship; it "puts in touch," just as Antoine Berman tells us translation does.

Here, the objection might be raised that even if we disregard any reference to primitivism, far from being mediators, these avant-garde artists were *appropriators*, a neologism that reminds us that we live in a period particularly sensitive to "cultural appropriation." Granting them the status of intercessors would therefore acknowledge their right to ownership over the meaning of works that therefore would not have any, or would no longer have any, of their own. In this way, the value of classical African masks would lie solely in the fact that they gave their faces to *Les Demoiselles d'Avignon*.

A systematic defiance toward anything that might resemble cultural appropriation may call into question the notion of an ethics of translation. On this point, the philosopher Kwame Anthony Appiah remarks, and with good reason, that quite often this concept is "misbegotten" and that "it wrongly casts cultural practices as something like corporate intellectual property." On the contrary, real offense caused toward the other's culture is caused only, he explains, when there is a lack of respect.[16] As for the avant-gardes' mediation, there was a real effort of translation. Nothing better exemplifies how these artists applied themselves respectfully to the *task of the translators* of African arts than the patience with which André Derain practiced sketching "primitive" works, particularly from Oceania, during his 1906 visit to the British Museum in London, and particularly in the ethnographic section. His task was to make his hand move his pencil as if it were imbued with the objects' visual language.

In a highly impactful article, Simon Gikandi condemned the fact that the artists of the avant-garde, Picasso in particular, effectively showed not the slightest respect when, while they were translating the visual language of artifacts coming from this continent, they showed at best a profound indifference for the "real" Africa behind its works of art.[17] Philippe Dagen also evokes the following "paradox": "Admiring 'Negro art' and despising Africans: this paradox may well prove to be persistent, however troublesome that observation may be for the elegant history of modern art such as it is most often told."[18]

Part of why Simon Gikandi's article had such an impact is that it constitutes an eloquent response to the 1984 event that was the exhibition *"Primitivism" in 20th Century Art: Affinity of the Tribal and the Modern* at the Museum of Modern Art in New York, curated by William Rubin, as well as the impressive catalog accompanying it, by the same name.[19] It was a response to two presuppositions of an art history that, on one hand, seeks to "minimize . . . the constitutive role of Africa in the making of modernism"[20] and, on the other hand, contends that the impact of these objects on an artist such as Picasso was above all psychological, that it was the effect of "forces" that they contain and that operate in a "subliminal" or "unconscious" manner rather than through true "intertextual" work.[21]

Undoubtedly, Picasso's own account of the impact that his 1906 visit to the Trocadéro museum had on him could favor situating his relationship to these objects on a strictly physical plane. He says the following regarding the gaze the masks fixed upon him, mirroring the gaze he fixed upon them:

> When I went to the old Trocadéro, it was revolting. The flea market. The odor. I was all alone. I wanted to leave. I didn't. I stayed. I stayed. I understood that it was very important: there was something happening to me, wasn't there? The masks weren't just sculptures like any other. Not at all. They were things of magic.[22]

What Simon Gikandi expresses in his critique of these two presuppositions, which are clearly related, especially as they appear in the article "Picasso," authored by William Rubin,[23] is that any psychological impact must not eclipse the work of translation.

The notion of the "dark forces" contained in these objects perpetuates the ethnographic theory according to which they are "fetishes" rather than works of art and thus could not possibly have any "meaning" by virtue of their visible form, divorced of the ritual contexts in which the ceremonial function that constitutes their entire being can be deployed. The moment they are deterritorialized, they no longer "speak" but may, as "forces," infiltrate the artistic unconscious, upon which it is incumbent to give them a real expression.

## THE DANCE OF MUTANTS

This is not to say that the language of "forces" cannot be used to describe the influences behind these objects. Quite the contrary. Such philosophers as William Emmanuel Abraham of Ghana and Léopold Sédar Senghor of Senegal insisted that, beyond the differences that exist from one region to the other within the continent, there exists a common denominator to Africa's arts: their commitment to abstraction, to diverging from a mere reproduction of reality, and their ambition to thus translate a different approach to reality, knowing it to be a universe of forces, of *élan vital*, to use a Bergsonian concept.

Consequently, the work that the artist creates is "religious," firstly because it pertains to the vital knowledge of reality as a creative flux. The object recapitulates within itself this flux that has given it life. It translates, therefore, as an *intercessor*, the movement that uplifts "inferior" forces of the assembled materials toward the emergent superior force of their composition, toward what Senghor calls "the light of the spirit."

> Rhythm is the vibrating shock, the power that, through the senses, seizes us at the roots of our *Being*. It expresses itself through the most material and sensual means: lines, surfaces, colors, and volumes in architecture, sculpture, and painting; accents in poetry and music; movements in dance. But, in doing this, it organizes all this concreteness toward the light of the *Spirit*.[24]

The stylized, geometric forms that the sculptor assembles converge in order to demonstrate the existence of an "ordering force" that holds them together in its "rhythm." The creation of a work of art is therefore the religious act of bringing forth a spiritual force out of material forces. To insistently claim that African artifacts are not "art" because their reason for being is their ritual function is to ignore that what makes them "religious" or "spiritual" is not, first and foremost, the role that they might play in ceremonies, but the *poiesis* by which they were begotten, by virtue of which they are fully and eminently works of art.

Hence they are not speech but speak the language of their forms, which they offered to the avant-gardes to translate. They have remained life forces, active in the creation of artistic modernity. I call them *mutants*, keeping in mind that this word comes from the present participle of the Latin verb *to change*, indicating that they are not the result of a metamorphosis whose aim is entirely exterior to them, but metamorphosis itself, still in the course of operating as the manifestation of the vital force.[25]

Concerning the "minimization" of their role in modernity, Simon Gikandi is right to highlight that it demonstrates "the struggle for a pure Picasso, one uncontaminated by Africa."[26] Are we, for that reason, to impute upon the avant-gardes, and upon Picasso in particular, a lack of "respect" for Africa? Gikandi devotes a large part of his analysis to displaying a Picasso who would never have truly shed his "Andalousian" way of considering Africa of the "Moors" as entirely "other," thereby putting in perspective his commitment to the continent's emancipation, despite his relationship with the "intercessors" that were the creations of African art.

One could respond that based on his biography, his actions, and his friendships, while the Andalousian in question was no Jean-Paul Sartre nor a "suitcase carrier,"[27] he was no less a man committed to liberation, alongside, for instance, the intellectual anticolonial movement that grew out of the publishing house Présence Africaine. Ultimately, though, the issue is above all that respect, it bears repeating, lies within the work of translation itself, of which it is the condition and motivating force.

This is why the avant-gardes who incorporated African art into their works, thereby demonstrating the roots they put down in the "country to which they were taken," likewise made a gesture of reciprocity: let us say the word, a decolonizing gesture. It is not naive to assess it as such. It is, on the contrary, a decision to refuse a cynical reading of the work of translation, one that is blind to its essence: generosity and hospitality.

Could one still say that these translator-mediators were lacking the very meaning of what they were translating out of ignorance of the territories in which they were made? For Amadou-Mahtar M'Bow, if they were traitors, it is, per the well-known Italian expression—*traduttore traditore*—for having translated. We know all too well that there is always some "resistance" from the work to be translated, and that the mediator "encounters it, at a very early stage, as the presumption of non-translatability, which inhibits him even before he tackles the work."[28] And the work of translation, which Paul Ricœur refers to as a "drama," is also one of mourning that accepts the impossibility of "filling the gap between equivalence and total adequacy," all while savoring "the pleasure of receiving the foreigner's word at home, in one's own welcoming house."[29]

## THE INTERCESSORS' INTERMINABLE VOYAGE

To return to the question of restitution, it should be quite clear that the objects' language will remain the "foreigner's word," even once returned, for those who welcome them, to their "country of origin." There are still, of course, specific objects that fill certain specific functions and whose departure opened a chasm waiting to be closed by them. They will find this empty space waiting. Does this likewise mean that they will reassume the meaning they initially held, as if their deterritorialization had never taken place?

This question has often been raised, but in a perverse sense, one might say, by numerous European museum directors during Africa's long "struggle for its art." For them, it was a way of resisting the slightest hope for restitution by claiming that ethnic groups, who alone were in a legitimate position to reclaim the artworks that their cultures had created, could have undergone profound changes such that they would no longer recognize these objects. If they had become Christian or Muslim, for example, they could even be opposed to the "returning" of creations that they no longer saw as anything but... "fetishes."

In response to the question thus posed and to this revival of the language of colonial ethnology, the Felwine Sarr and Bénédicte Savoy report rightly points out that artworks held as such in European museums would likewise be returned as such to states, not to ethnic groups. It would then be up to African nations to "resocialize" them, to use the authors' word, in the way they best saw fit.

Resocialization will call for retranslation.

Sculptures of classical African art, when returned to "their own homes," will speak a language made up of many hybridizations, which will require translating. The translation that is their return does not undo the translation that was their departure; it adds to it. Like Derain visiting the ethnographic galleries of the British Museum, African artists who wish to converse with works of art of the past will have to learn to translate them, to train their hand and pencil so as to learn how to incorporate them, perhaps, into new creations.

The South African artist Ernest Mancoba (1904–2002) was trained in this way, in Anglican schools, in wood sculpture in the most classical of Western tradition. Among the most famous of his naturalist works, his 1929 *Bantu Madonna* bears witness to this education. It was in 1936 that he encountered "Negro art," and, as reports a newspaper article dedicated to his work, he "ceased to follow European styles of sculpture and art" after having "discovered the negro art of Africa" in order to "[apply] it with enthusiasm to his own conceptions."[30] For the classical art of central Africa was, for him as well, a "discovery," an encounter with a language that he had to learn to translate.[31]

Fidelity to cultural heritage will come through the movement of translating it.

In short, translation continues, and, like Odysseus returning to Ithaca, it will not remain in one place; the odyssey of objects that have become "diasporic"[32] will see no end. From here on, it is in their nature to belong equally to their different "countries," with those countries where they are no longer present always missing them. In a general way, beyond art, it is important today to recall that heritage is shared, that it serves not to glorify identities but to open them to a common humanity. This is why, once they are legally repatriated, returned African artworks will continue to come and go, to be like the birds that divide their time between Europe and Africa, spending winters here, summers there: migrants.

# 4.

# THE PHILOSOPHER AS TRANSLATOR

◆

> A decolonized university in Africa should put African languages at the center of its teaching and learning project. Colonialism rhymes with monolingualism. The African university of tomorrow will be multilingual. It will teach (in) Swahili, isiZulu, isiXhosa, Shona, Yoruba, Hausa, Lingala, Gikuyu and it will teach all those other African languages French, Portuguese or Arabic have become, while making a space for Chinese, Hindi etc.[1]
>
> —ACHILLE MBEMBE

## PHILOSOPHY OF GRAMMAR

In 1958, Émile Benveniste published an article entitled "Categories of Thought and Language" in the journal *Les Études philosophiques* in which he made two significant philosophical moves.[2] The first was to question, from a linguist's point of view, the very foundation of Western metaphysics, based as it was on the Aristotelian doctrine of categories. The second was to compare (that is, once again, to place together on equal footing) Greek and Ewe as bearing two different "metaphysics of being."[3]

This questioning lay in the article's thesis, which claimed that when Aristotle enumerates the list of universal "categories" that, according to him, structure our experience, that is, the "totality of predications that may be made about a being," he is merely "identifying certain fundamental categories of the language in which he thought,"[4] namely, Greek. This thesis challenges the universality of categories of being and thought by reducing them to the Greek language and its specific grammar.

Benveniste cites a passage of the Aristotelian treatise *Categories* (chapter 4) that he calls "fundamental" and that he "translated literally." Then, in his commentary, he suggests that if "substance" is the category that in response to the question of *what?* offers a noun, "quantity" the one that answers the question of *how much?*, and so on for "quality" (the question of *what kind?*), "relation" (the question of *relative to what?*), "place" (the question of *where?*), "time" (the question of *when?*), "position" (the question of *to be in a position*?), "state" (the question of *to be in a condition?*), "action" (the question *to do?*), and "passion" (the question of *to undergo?*), it is because these predications are not "attributes discovered in things" but rather correspond to a classification "arising from the language itself,"[5] in which are found a class of nouns, a class of adjectives derived from pronouns, comparative adjectives, adverbs of place and time, active and passive voices...

After demonstrating that these categories of being were linguistic in nature, and thus relative to the Greek language, Benveniste examines "being," or "the being," itself, which he says "envelops everything" and "without being a predicate itself... is the condition of all predicates."[6] Greek contains a verb *to be* that plays the role of the copula when a predicate P is attributed to a subject S, yielding a proposition of the form "S is P." Furthermore, an article can turn the verb, as in French for example, into a noun when it stays in the infinitive form, while in other "copular" languages, this nominalization is carried out through the present participle. In this sense, quite a few Indo-European languages therefore have an equivalent of *being*.

Nietzsche, then, was right to say:

> The strange family resemblance of all Indian, Greek, and German philosophizing is explained easily enough. Where there is affinity of languages, it cannot fail, owing to the common philosophy of grammar—I mean, owing to the unconscious domination and guidance by similar grammatical functions—that everything is prepared at the outset for a similar development and sequence of philosophical systems; just as the way seems barred against certain other possibilities of world-interpretation.[7]

Indian, Greek, and German philosophy have in common their expression in Indo-European languages, and it is precisely in order to contrast them with "other possibilities of world-interpretation" that Émile Benveniste raises the issue of a "metaphysics of being" not based on the word *being* or on its usage in copular languages.

Before examining the decentering by way of Ewe, "a language of an entirely different type"[8] that the linguist carries out, we should recall the philosophical objections that were raised against what seems to reduce all philosophy to its particular language (rather than, simply, to language), and primarily Jacques Derrida's response to what appear to him to be "the aporias which one seems to encounter once one sets out to define the constraints which limit philosophical discourse."[9]

For one, he says, when one thus places *linguistic categories* and *categories of thought* face-to-face, knowing that thought could not simply be the matter to which language gives form, one acts "as if" it were the case. Derrida also reminds us that the question is not new and that "productions of language have long been specifically recognized in [Aristotle's] categories."[10] Here he cites, among the various works that preceded Benveniste's article, the 1846 study by Friedrich Adolf Trendelenberg, and more recently that of Léon Brunschvicg in *Les Âges de l'intelligence.* In regard to these works, Derrida says that they could even be seen as having been paraphrased in "Categories of Thought and Language."

## *TRANSLATIO STUDII*

To measure what categories of thought owe to the "philosophy of grammar" inherent in a language is to submit it to "the trial of the foreign," or, in other words, of translation. One could add that this trial would be all the more instructive the further the languages, that which is translated and that which receives, are apart. Indeed, Cicero, for instance, found himself feeling intimidated by the task of translating concepts he had learned to conceptualize in Greek into his Roman language, even after having set aside objections both from those who disapproved of the very study of philosophy itself and from those who believed that such a pursuit could be carried out only in the native idiom of Plato and Aristotle. Regarding the latter, in particular, Cicero maintained that welcoming the "transcendent intellects" (*divina illa ingenia*) that were the Greek thinkers in Latin, to make them familiar to his fellow citizens, was above all a service to be provided for them.[11]

Upon rereading Cicero's reflections on the undertaking of translating Greek philosophy into Latin, it is hard to imagine that the choices he put forth for new words (for example, the word *qualitas* as the equivalent of *poiótēs* to translate the category of "quality") struck his contemporaries as incongruous: for we know that these words later became standard concepts and that, generally speaking, it was the *translatio studii*, or the transfer, from one culture to another, from one language to another, of Greek thought that made Latin the language of philosophy par excellence in Europe, and for centuries, at that.

Ultimately, there was not the slightest reason for Cicero's concerns before the task of translating. Latin shared with Greek, the language of the philosophy it was receiving, a "common philosophy of grammar," to return to Nietzsche's remark. To model *qualitas*, something's "what-ness" after *poiótēs*, is to carry out, from one language to another, an operation analogous to that which allowed the Greeks to pass from the interrogative "*poîos*" (*of what kind?*) to the abstract term that describes the quality of the thing in question. And there are certainly analogous "possibilities" allowed for by similar usages of the verb *to be*. Translating Aristotelian metaphysics of being from Greek to the language of Rome was, in quite a few ways, less so a trial of the foreign as it was an experiment in a "common philosophy of grammar."

What Émile Benveniste sought to carry out in his 1958 article was a true decentering, by way of "confrontation," he says, with a language "of an entirely different type," such as Ewe, in which "the notion of 'to be,' or what we shall designate as such, is divided among several verbs."[12] He was undoubtedly unaware that in the tenth century CE, translations of Greek philosophy into Arabic were already raising the same question that he posed, that of the relationship between Aristotle's logical categories and the categories of his language.

The *translatio studii* does not refer solely to the path, to which it is too often reduced, leading from Greek to Latin and later to its Europe descendants. It equally accounts for the translation of Greek philosophy from Greek into Syriac and Arabic. We should recall, here, the description given of the *translatio studii* by Roger Bacon:

> God first revealed philosophy to his saints and gave them the laws . . . It was thus primarily and most completely given in the Hebrew language. It was then renewed in the Greek language, primarily by Aristotle; then in the Arabic language, primarily through Avicenna; but it was never composed in Latin and was only translated/transferred (*translata*) based on foreign languages, and the best [texts] are not translated.[13]

It is important to pay particular attention to this remark, which demonstrates how a thirteenth-century author such as Roger Bacon could attach considerable importance to the translation/transfer of Greek thought into Arabic (more so than into Latin, as we can observe here), thereby deconstructing the fabrication of a history of philosophy as a purely and exclusively European affair having begun as a "Greek miracle." We must keep in mind that it was in fact, as Roger-Pol Droit writes, only "recently, in an almost sudden way," that philosophy "was conceived of as being solely Greek."[14] It was in the nineteenth and especially twentieth centuries, Droit reminds us, that "this modern myth of philosophy as Greek and Greek alone"[15] was established, then taught by textbooks, which would have the Logos be a feature of the West. This myth was born of colonialism.[16]

Regarding the relationship between colonialism and the prestige of philosophy, we must recall that the translations of Greek philosophers into Latin, on one hand, and Arabic, on the other, have the following in common: they were carried out in languages that were in no position to be considered as peripheral in relation to the "hypercenter." Latin was the language of the Roman Empire. Arabic was the language not only of the Muslim Empire but also, and most importantly, of Revelation. And it was from this place of "hypercentrality" that grammarians of the latter language have reproached philosopher-translators of Aristotle for trying to pass off as categories of thought in a broad sense what were merely the categories inherent in the language spoken by the Stagirite.

This dispute over languages and their translation in the Islamic world was embodied, dramatized, we might say, in the form of a public debate that took place in Baghdad in the year 932, which pitted the philosopher-logician Abu Bishr Matta ibn Yunus against the grammarian Abu Said al-Sirafi on the topic of the universality of Aristotelian categories and logic. This philosophical sparring match, oft cited by historians of Islamic philosophy, warrants a place among the classic texts of philosophy of translation.[17]

The scene is mostly dedicated to expressing the grammarian's wrath in the face of what happens to the language of Revelation when Arab philosophers dare to offer hospitality in their language to what the Greeks, who were yet ignorant of the one God, called "love of wisdom." Indeed, for guardians of the language, nothing better demonstrates this imposture than the very name of these philosophers, these *falāsifa* (sing. *faylasūf*), an Arabization of the Greek *philosophia*, effectively showing that their wisdom is foreign to Arabic and to Islam.

Al-Sirafi's wrath is aimed at the inevitable hybridizations that translation had imposed upon the language. We can easily imagine, in the same way that the Latin *quid-ditas* seemed at first to be an ill-suited neologism for translating essence, *ousia*, a structurally equivalent neologism such as *māhiyah* in Arabic would have irritated grammarian purists. This is a word, later turned into a philosophical concept, that was constructed, as it happens, in the process of translation, on the model of *qualitas* or *quidditas*. Just as, from the word *quid*, which asks the question *what?*, the abstract *quidditas* was created in Latin, which became *quiddity* in English, so too does the word *mā*, for questioning something's nature, produce, by adjoining the suffix *-iyah*, which functions here as *-itas*, *-ity*, or *-ness*, the concept *māhiyah* to mean something's "essence," otherwise stated, its "what-it-is-ness."

In his confrontation with the philosopher Matta, the grammarian al-Sirafi's target is above all Aristotle's logic translated into Arabic. He vehemently denounces the fact that these *falāsifa* accept the idea that the Stagirite's *Organon* teaches a universal logic, thus ignoring the logic of their own language, inherent in its grammar. He considers them at once ignorant of the language (he accordingly gives his philosophical interlocutor, with great delight, several "tests" to highlight the latter's linguistic shortcomings) and traitors to it.

The conflict is between the idea that every language has its own particular logic and the idea that there is one logic that is the instrument of reasoning in general, whose categories of thought owe nothing to the language in which they are expressed. Al-Sirafi's rebuke of Hellenizing philosophers is that they are unaware that translation is a diminishment, that the transfer of Aristotle's logic first into Syriac and then into Arabic (as the first translations of Greek philosophy were initially based on the Syriac) signified that it was doubly removed from the truth of the original. To this, Abu Bishr Matta responds that the work of translation conserves the universal, or, even better: that the universal is precisely what is conserved in translation. Therefore, while it so happens that the universal grammar of reasoning was transmitted to us in Greek, then in Syriac, it in fact transcends these languages.

While the wrath that he continuously displays during the debate hardly renders the arrogant grammarian sympathetic, nor does it blind him to the truth of the position he upholds, that the universal must be grounded in the plurality of languages, that none of them is the Logos incarnate by which all others must be measured. There was Babel, and so, from that point on, the universal must be forged and experienced through human languages, all of them, "imperfect insofar as they are many," in the words of Mallarmé, and through the encounter between them that is translation.

It is not irrelevant that Arabic is not, like Greek, a "copular" language once one is aware of the significance of the canonical "S is P" formulation of the statement that, for Aristotle, attributes a predicate to a subject. Therefore, when such philosophers as Matta suggest adopting in Arabic a formulation that would be more ordinary for that language, such as "Socrates, him, philosopher," having the personal pronoun *him* play the role filled by the copula *is* in Greek, the "ontological" character of a predicate's *inherence* in a subject is turned into the logical *relationship* between two terms.

Therefore, rather than showing that the quality of philosopher is inscribed, as an attribute, within the very essence of Socrates, the relationship established by the personal pronoun *him* indicates that the individual "Socrates" belongs to the class of those who possess the property "philosopher."

To return to Benveniste's demonstration, it was only normal that it should revolve around the translation of the verb *to be* in Ewe. To "pit" this language against Greek was significant in more ways than one.

First, to raise the question of a metaphysics of being in this language, even rhetorically, undeniably had a political as well as philosophical significance. Such an affirmation of the *comparability* of Greek and Ewe, that is, the possibility of placing them together as equals, on the same plane, was in line with the decolonial atmosphere of the time.

This period, namely, saw the Bandung conference of 1955 condemn the very principle of any colonization and affirm the existence of a world with a plurality of cultures and languages, all of equal dignity for giving different outlooks on the human adventure. Bandung was, in its way, a repetition of the myth of Babel. To test Greek categories against those of Ewe, to carry out such a decentering of the prestigious ancestral Logos, ultimately meant bringing its heir, the language of colonization, down from its pedestal, compared with which a vernacular such as Ewe could only ever be incomplete and lacking: like all other non-(Indo-) European vernaculars, it had no abstract terms, it had no future tense, and, most of all, it had no verb *to be*.

Jean-Pierre Lefebvre gave the term *ontological nationalism* to the preconception that philosophy is monolingual, speaking only Greek yesterday, German today, as well as perhaps, in a pinch, their (Indo-)European cousins that share similar usages of the words for *to be*, *being*, etc.[18]

It is against this preconception of "native" vernaculars as defined by what they lack that the linguist Benveniste implies in his article that no language is "incomplete," in any respect,[19] and explicitly posits that, especially when it comes to the word upon which the ontological tradition in (Indo-)European languages has been constructed, quite far from lacking a verb *to be*, Ewe is, if anything . . . overflowing.

Commenting on Diedrich Westermann's work on this language,[20] Benveniste notes that the French *être* ("to be"), for example, "is divided among several verbs":

—A verb *nyé*, which he says "states, 'to be someone, to be something,'" and thus "serves to equate subject and predicate."

—A verb *le*, which states existence and is employed to assert that "God exists" (*Mawu le*). Apart from this intransitive, absolute use, it also takes predicates that tell location, situation, state, etc. . . . in these cases *le* is in the aorist.

—If the statement is in a different tense, then the transitive verb *no*, meaning "to remain, to stay," is used.

—A verb *wo*, "to do, to accomplish, to produce an effect," which "behaves in the manner of our 'to be' followed by an adjective denoting substance": thus *wo* followed by the word meaning "sand" expresses "to be sandy," followed by the word used to say "water" expresses "to be wet," etcetera.

—Finally, a verb *du*, which is used when the predicate "is a term of function or of rank," as in "to be king."[21]

The linguist then makes the important remark that it is only through an "egocentric comparison"[22] that one could consider these five verbs as different possibilities for translating the verb "to be" in French. From the point of view of Ewe, nothing could bring them together under one single umbrella: they are quite simply different.

This effectively demonstrates that in what would be an Ewe "metaphysics," the notion of *being* would be entirely different.

## DECOLONIZING, TRANSLATING

What the French linguist put forth at the time as a hypothesis, as a thought experiment, had taken further shape in the work of Rwandan philosopher Alexis Kagamé (1912–1981). In a dissertation that he presented in 1955—three years, that is, before the publication of Benveniste's article—on Bantu-Rwandan philosophy of being, Abbot Kagamé raised the same premise as the linguist did, that of categories of thought depending on categories of language, and drew the same conclusions from it. With these conclusions at his disposal, he then studied the "philosophy of grammar" of the language Kinyarwanda so as to unearth its linguistic and grammatical categories and arrange them in a table, in the same way as Aristotle.[23]

In the fifth chapter of a second work of comparative Bantu philosophy, dedicated to showing the "difference between Bantu Ontology and that," he says, "which we have absorbed in the Europeans' School,"[24] Kagamé declares that for Bantus, "the one genus" is "being-*ntu*." *Ntu*, he writes, "= being, or something," establishing that it corresponds to "*being* in Europeo-American philosophy."[25] Consequently, the questions *what . . . ?* and *what about . . . ?* are answered depending on the categories of language that determine *ntu*. The determinations are as follows:

—The prefix *mu* adjoined to *ntu* gives *muntu*, meaning "man." The plural form is *bantu*. Determination by *mu* thus produces the category of existents endowed with intelligence.

—When the prefix is *ki*, its combination with *ntu* gives *kintu*, meaning "thing." *Bintu*, then, the plural of *kintu*, expresses "things," existents without intelligence.

—A third prefix, *ha*, added to *ntu* produces the category *hantu*, which determines the existent's location in space and time.

—Finally, a fourth prefix, *ku*, gives *kuntu* (a form, Kagamé specifies, which is "only used in interlacustrine Africa, other linguistic Bantu zones using other resources of the language"), which determines the existent's way or mode of being.

The full table of categories of Bantu ontology is presented as follows:

MUntu = intelligent existent (*man*)
KIntu = existent-without-intelligence (*thing*)
HAntu = locating existent (*place-time*)
KUntu = modal existent (*existent's way of being*)[26]

In 1982, Paulin Hountondji criticized Abbot Alexis Kagamé's *La Philosophie bantu-rwandaise de l'être* (Bantu-Rwandan philosophy of being), seeing in it the depiction "of a treacherous theological approach that was historically and still remains, for many Africans, a formidable temptation."[27] I, personally, would say that the temptation is that of imprisonment in an *ntu-logical nationalism*. What does one actually gain, desiring to be at all costs different from that which "we have absorbed in the Europeans' School," by undertaking with the Bantu *ntu* a simple tracing of what was done with the Greek *on*?

There is much talk today of "decolonizing," especially of "the mind,"[28] in a great many academic and cultural fields and disciplines. It is certainly necessary, but what does it mean?

Kagamé's procedure, which falls under what I have termed an ethnology of difference, gives *decolonize* a relativist and separatist meaning: philosophies are, for him, separate systems of thought, formed by radically different languages and grammatical philosophies. Against the very idea of translation, he writes the following:

> In Europeo-American philosophy [. . .] *to be* is synonymous with *to exist*, and *being* with *existent*. But it is not the same in Bantu Philosophy. Here, the verb *to be* plays only the role of *copula*, and must, consequently, be accompanied by

> a complement or an adverbial phrase of place. The famous formula: *I think therefore I am* has no meaning in Bantu languages. Listeners would inquire: *you are... what*—or: *you are... where.*[29]

It is understood that while he is confident regarding the cartesian *cogito* in Bantu, it is because Kagamé has in mind a word in Kinyarwanda that could translate *to be*, but not in the absolute, intransitive way in which it is used there. Nevertheless, it is the assertion that "I think therefore I am" has no meaning in a Bantu language that itself has no meaning. Or rather, that is a misinterpretation of the idea of translation.

Does the Rwandan philosopher actually mean to say that one can fully *understand* the statement in Latin, reading the *Meditationes*, or in French, reading *Le Discours de la méthode*, but that it is impossible to translate into a Bantu language or any other of African origin, in which the verb *to be* "plays only the role of copula"? Or rather, does he mean to say that one could find a way of translating it, but that this translation would make no sense? Upon further reflection, these two possibilities are one and the same.

George Steiner opened his work *After Babel* with a chapter that argued for "Understanding as Translation."[30] We are always able to find a way to convey a statement (perhaps to be polished later, in another translation...) precisely because this transfer into another language continues the *movement* of the translation that is my initial understanding of that statement. Does Kagamé believe that the static statement, taken as an isolate, "I think therefore I am" made, as such, more sense in French when first written in that language than in Bantu? It has meaning not because of the way we speak in French, but rather because it was the conclusion of a series of moves that effectively made it a de facto exception to the evil genius hypothesis. It is everything that comes before the moment I tell the evil genius that "he can trick me as much as he pleases, he can never make it such that I am not, as long as I am thinking..." that gives meaning to "I think, therefore I am," independent of whether the argument is stated in French, Latin, or a Bantu language.

What makes the cogito a philosophical concept is that it is the conclusion of a demonstration. This is why it is always translatable and makes sense in translation, even if we can indeed call it an "untranslatable," in the sense that Barbara Cassin gives the word at numerous points of her body of work: "That which one never stops (not) translating."[31]

I counter the relativist and separatist model of decolonizing thought with a translational model. Since languages do not imprison us within incommensurable grammatical philosophies, the philosopher in general, and the African philosopher in particular, shall think like a translator, from language to language. Such is the practice, for instance, of Ghanaian philosopher Kwasi Wiredu, who, while calling African philosophers to work in African languages, also shows the interest in coming and going between English and Akan so as to submit philosophical arguments and concepts to *the trial of the foreign*.[32]

In the reflection he offers on "the concept of truth in the Akan language,"[33] Kwasi Wiredu explains that if we take the word *truth* in a cognitive sense, excluding the moral sense of "truthfulness," it then becomes, from the perspective of the West African idiom, an *untranslatable*. This observation is, by all appearances, analogous to that made by Kagamé regarding the cogito and Bantu. But Wiredu's aim is to test, by way of translation, such philosophical questions as a theory of truth as correspondence between a proposition and a state of affairs. He writes the following:

> The concepts of truth and fact are among the most fundamental concepts of human thought. Without the notion of something being a fact or of a proposition being true, thinking is inconceivable unless it be a mere succession of ideas, and even that can be doubted. It seems obvious, then, that the relation between the terms "truth" and "fact" is a philosophical issue; for, of course, one cannot give a fundamental clarification of either of these foundational concepts in English without relating them one to the other. Yet, since these terms need not both be present in all natural languages, as the case of Akan shows, this task is not inescapable for the human mind. From which it follows that some philosophical problems are not universal.[34]

Generally speaking, the space between languages allows one to step outside of the imprisonment of any single one of them, which is the final lesson of Benveniste's reflection on "Categories of Thought and Language":

> No type of language can by itself alone foster or hamper the activity of the mind. The advance of thought is linked much more closely to the capacities of men, to general conditions of culture and to the organization of society than to the particular nature of a language.[35]

# 5.
# TRANSLATING THE WORD OF GOD

◆

> Translation is 'impossible' concedes Ortega y Gasset in his *Miseria y esplendor de la traducción*. But so is all absolute concordance between thought and speech. Somehow the 'impossible' is overcome at every moment in human affairs.[1]
>
> —GEORGE STEINER

LET US BEGIN WITH a reading of the first pages of Cheikh Hamidou Kane's novel *Ambiguous Adventure*,[2] which from the moment it came out in 1961 became a great classic of world literature. The book's opening scene, in which we see students at a Quranic school learning to recite the "word of God" under the tutelage of Thierno,[3] their schoolmaster, is famous. It begins as follows:

> That day, Thierno had beaten him again. And yet Samba Diallo knew his sacred verse. It was only that he had made a slip of the tongue. Thierno had jumped up as if he had

> stepped on one of the white-hot paving stones of the gehenna promised to evil-doers. He had seized Samba Diallo by the fleshy part of his thigh and, between his thumb and index finger, had given him a long hard pinch. The child had gasped with pain and begun to shake all over. Threatened by sobs which were strangling him in the chest and throat, he had had the strength to master his suffering; in a weak voice, broken and stammering, but correctly, he had repeated the verse from the holy Book which he had spoken badly in the first place.[4]

We then learn that the schoolmaster is capable of going as far as pinching the child's ear until it bleeds, or scorching them with a burning log! The alarm this violence causes becomes complete when the narrator brings us into Thierno's thoughts, where we discover that the treatment he inflicts on the child is not cruelty on his part per se, but a direct result of the tyrannic love he has for him. His attachment and admiration for the boy are profound, as he sees in him "a gift from God" promised for the heights of "human grandeur."[5]

For precisely this reason, Thierno does not allow the child the right to the slightest error:

> Be accurate in repeating the Word of your Lord. He has done you the gracious favor of bringing His own speech down to you. These words have been veritably pronounced by the Master of the World. And you, miserable lump of earthy mold that you are, when you have the honor of repeating them after Him, you go so far as to profane them by your carelessness.[6]

And the boy, as the text tells us, is in fervent agreement: "it was a word come from God, it was a miracle" and the "sentence—which he did not understand, for which he was suffering martyrdom—he loved for its mystery and its somber beauty."

This scene from the first pages of *Ambiguous Adventure* raises the theological and philosophical question of what it means to be the "miracle" of a word "come from God" and "veritably pronounced" by Him. It likewise raises the question of the significance of reciting "the Word" without understanding it because its language is foreign, or rather, if one can appreciate the child's attitude, of understanding it *lovingly* in its very mystery. It raises the issue of what I call, on one hand, *vertical translation* of the word of God, which is the "descent" of the infinite and the eternal into the finitude and temporality of human language, and on the other hand, the *horizontal translations* of this word, when it is rendered in other human languages, such as Fulani, spoken by Samba Diallo and his schoolmaster Thierno.[7]

In this case, does horizontal translation signify a loss of being for the meaning of the divine word in the movement of transfer from its sacred language (hypercentrality being sanctity, in this case) toward one that is peripheral or profane? Pursuing this question further, one could ask if the sanctity of a language is one of its essential characteristics, to remain for all eternity, predisposing it to welcoming the divine word, or if it is, on the contrary, this election that gives it its newfound status, apart from which it is simply a human language among others, all "imperfect insofar as they are many." Could horizontal translation, then, transfer some of the sanctity of the language that initially received Revelation to the welcoming language?

## THEOLOGY OF VERTICAL TRANSLATION

In what sense is the sacred text the word of God? This question is raised in the three "religions of the Book," to use the term that, in Islam, denotes Judaism and Christianity and that is applied just as well, and even more so, to the Muslim religion. This theological and philosophical question gives the twelfth chapter of Spinoza's *Theologico-Political Treatise* its title: "Of the true original of the divine law, and wherefore scripture is called sacred, and the word of God. How that, in so far as it contains the word of God, it has come down to us uncorrupted."[8]

At the start of this chapter, Spinoza addresses "those who look upon the Bible as a message sent down by God from Heaven to men" to tell them that "the original of the covenant which God made with the Jews has been lost." He adds, "Not only reason but the expressed opinions of prophets and apostles openly proclaim that God's eternal Word and covenant, no less than true religion, is Divinely inscribed in human hearts, that is, in the human mind, and that this is the true original of God's covenant."[9]

An essential consequence of this thesis is that Scripture is sacred and its teachings divine so long as it lives in "human hearts." Should it be neglected, should it become a literal dead letter, the degradation thereof would prevent it from being discussed in these terms, leaving it only to be idolized as ink and paper.

The vertical translation of the word of God can take place only, as Spinoza says, if it is incorporated in humans. There it is made a living and lived word, living because it is lived. Only when it is made manifest in devotion does it truly become "written by the very hand of God." Otherwise, it is susceptible to corruption, like everything that enters into the sensible world. In the time of Jeremy, Spinoza explains, it was false to call the structure that perished in flames the temple of God, as it had already been deserted by the believers. In the same way, tablets bearing a law that is not respected are nothing but stone blocks. Otherwise, how are we to believe that Moses, even at the height of his fury before spectacles of impiety, could have thrown and shattered them if they truly carried words drawn on them by God Himself? To this significant theological question, Spinoza responds: because it was no longer the word of God, but rather ephemeral inscriptions on stone tablets that could be destroyed.

In fact, the word of God cannot be received but by that which is of its same nature: the heart of the believer. Such is how we are to understand the prophetic word in Islam that makes God proclaim that neither His earth nor His sky can contain Him, but that the heart of the faithful servant can—the heart, or what Muslim philosophers have called intellect or prophetic faculty.

To say that vertical translation is the reception of the divine word by a human language is to say, in Platonic terms, that, from the realm of the divine and of the intelligible, the word "descends" into the sensible realm of language, in which its uncreated nature becomes adorned with created words, and in which its eternity becomes our temporality.

"Descent" (*tanzīl*) is one name for the Quran. Thus it is the descent, all at once, of Revelation into the heart of the prophet of Islam, who was illiterate, as tradition teaches us. In other words, his very heart was immaculacy itself, a blank slate ready to receive that which is "written by the very hand of God" in one fell swoop. But Revelation is also the time it took to be translated into Arabic, the twenty-three years over the course of which it unfolded, fragment after fragment, verse after verse, literally coming from the prophetic body. It is, therefore, simultaneously a fiat produced in one sole moment, outside of time, and a twenty-three-year translation into the sounds, letters, and words that were assembled to form the Quranic text.

The Quran can be considered a witness to its own construction in the movement of "descent" through the isolated letters placed at the beginning of certain chapters, to which it is impossible to give any meaning. The second chapter begins in this way, with the letters *a*, *l*, and *m*, pronounced *alif*, *lam*, *mim*. The letters found at the beginning of chapter 20, *ta* and *ha*, can form a word, *taha*, which cannot be assigned any meaning, but which is traditionally interpreted as being a "name" for the prophet. For this reason, it is a commonplace name in the Islamic world. The same occurred with the letters *ya* and *sin* forming *yasin*, which open chapter 36.

Independent of the esoteric interpretations that may be suggested, we can read these isolated letters—which sometimes give the impression that their assembly into words is still underway, always in movement—as the meaning of what is signified by "descent" or vertical translation, that of an infinite word that is thus "neither sound nor letter,"[10] entering from the eternal into the temporal and the finitude of a human language. *Alif*, *lam*, *mim*, *ta*, *ha*, *ya*, *sin*, etcetera are therefore, in their isolation, still upon the threshold that separates the intelligible from its sensible translation, thereby witness to the fact that translation is not a petrification in tablets, but a movement still in the process of being carried out.

How, then, did Moses hear the word that God addressed to him? asked the theologian Abu Hamid al-Ghazali (1058–1111), romanized as Algazel, well known in West Africa, as throughout the Islamic world, where he is given the title Imam Ghazali. We cannot say, he continues, that he heard it in the form of "sound and letter"; and therefore the only answer is that he heard this eternal word in a manner that is inaccessible to us:

> The speech of God is written in books, memorized by hearts, and recited by tongues. The paper, ink, script, letters, and sounds are all occurrents, since they are bodies and modes [subsisting] in bodies, and all of these are occurrents. If we say that it—I mean the attribute of the Eternal—is written in the books, it does not follow that the eternal speech resides in the books. Just as we say that fire is written in a book, it does not follow from this that fire itself resides in the book. If fire resides in the book, it would be burned; and if fire itself resides in the tongue of someone who says "fire," his tongue would be burned [. . .] Similarly, eternal speech, which subsists in the essence of God, is what is indicated and not the indicator [. . .] Thus respecting the copies of the Qur'ān is obligatory, since they contain indicators of an attribute of God.[11]

As regards the distinction between the speech subsisting in the essence and the one written in books, we should note that the Quran, which is quite self-referential, puts forth the notion of a "mother of the Book," eternally remaining in God's presence. It seems to translate the idea that the womb that produced the word remains in the intelligible and eternal world from which the word "descends" to join the sensible and the temporal.[12]

Let us not, however, introduce a duality within a word that would remain its integral in the intelligible while casting its shadow, so to speak, on the created world of what is to come. The Quranic text itself insists that the Revelation of which it is comprised is perfected, that it has "descended" in its totality and that nothing was lost in vertical translation. Such is the position expressed with the firmest conviction by the Quranic school's teacher, Thierno, that "these words have been veritably pronounced by the Master of the World." This is the position adopted by literalists on the controversial theological question that has been raised starting from the last third of the seventh century in the Islamic world: that of knowing whether the Quran is the uncreated and eternal word of God, or if it is indeed His word but without sharing His divine eternity, having been created, on the contrary, in the human language in which it is embodied.

The rationalist position is the second possibility in the dichotomy presented here. We may observe that the previously cited passage from Ghazali is a response to this question, in which he expresses the idea that "what is indicated" is uncreated, whereas the indicator, made up of accidents, is created. This controversial position, a rationalism that could be qualified as moderate, is that of the Ashari theological school, of which Ghazali is at the forefront. It is distinguished from the rationalism of the school known as Mutazilite, which holds that the Quran was simply created, as well as from the Hanbali movement, which refuses all but the literalist assertion that the Quranic verses, word and speech, are such as the Master of the World pronounced them.

We shall note that the Jewish philosopher Maimonides also took part in this reflection on the word of God and its translation in human languages. It is the subject of his commentary in chapter 26 of *The Guide for the Perplexed* on the Talmudic maxim that declares that "the Torah speaks in the language of man." Revelation always exists as a translation in the language "of the children of Adam."

## POLITICS OF HORIZONTAL TRANSLATION

Indeed, Babel took place, and the "children of Adam" speak innumerable languages. What then is to become of the translation that we shall call *horizontal*, from human language to human language? This question is closely tied to that of the *sacred* nature of the language that welcomes Revelation, set aside from all others by this nature and status.

The questions of translatability and the relationship between the language considered sacred and vernacular languages is at the heart of Lamin Sanneh's work *Translating the Message: The Missionary Impact on Culture.*[13] The book by this Christian theologian, a specialist in the history of missions, essentially presents a comparison of the relationships that Islam and Christianity have with the translation of the word of God, particularly in the colonial African context. He emphasizes what he considers to be the force of Christianity, the fact of having faith in translatability and of being in the continuous movement of translation. Considering the historical counterexamples that could be offered against this assessment, he highlights that ultimately, translation has always prevailed over the reluctance toward the vernacularization of the message. The event of Pentecost, which saw crowds hearing the word of the apostles, everyone in their own language, proves that "Christianity is without a revealed language,"[14] he explains.

In the colonial world, Sanneh continues, it is important to note that the Christian religion fully assumed translatability and made it the weapon of missions: the message is translated into African languages, for example, as it always had been into the languages of the peoples who successively accepted it. In this way, the theologian then says, "The historian is thus confronted with a signal fact about Christianity in the sense that its continuous translatability left it as the only major world religion that is peripheral in the land of its origin."[15]

Lanneh subsequently insists quite particularly on two points. The first is that we must reject the idea that the mission aligned its actions with that of colonialism, pursuing the same end of negating the cultures and languages under its supervision. On the contrary, the theologian maintains, this being his second point, that missionary faith in translatability signifies the development and promotion of vernacular languages, which, as it happens, fostered anticolonial nationalism.

Sanneh establishes a contrast with Islam on all of these matters. He considers the "missionary institution" of Islam to be "the Qur'an school where little boys and girls memorize passages of the sacred book in Arabic. That, rather than scriptural translation, has been the mode of Islam's expansion throughout the world."[16] He thus highlights what one could call, to return to Pascale Casanova's analysis, a hypercentrality of Arabic in Muslim societies, which he writes have even fostered "an inferiority complex" toward that language as it is the "revealed language of Islam."[17] In this way he explains the absolute opposition, sanctioned by various legal schools, to a liturgical use, especially for canonical Muslim prayers, of any language other than Quranic speech in Arabic, even though it is not understood by the majority of believers. He likewise remarks, though, without explanation, that the "language barrier" has not hindered the expansion of Islam, which he calls "impressive," which would seem to suggest that "understanding the sacred text seems subordinate to venerating it."[18] The Samba Diallos of the Islamic world love the word, even if it is not (yet) translated, "for its mystery and its somber beauty."

Lanneh caricatures and exaggerates this contrast, which seeks to hold a Christian message, naturally open to translation, to interpretation, to updates and therefore to pluralism, up against an Islamic religion founded upon untranslatability and closed to the very idea of interpreting a word as it is, pronounced by God Himself. Is this the case?

As opposed to the biblical text, the Quran indeed has several times more references to its own language, describing itself, to take one among many possible examples, as follows: "And most surely this is a revelation from the Lord of the worlds. The Faithful Spirit has descended with it, upon your heart that you may be of the warners, in plain Arabic language."[19]

We should note that another verse (16:103) refers to those who deny that Muhammad received divine revelation and accuse him of recounting the teachings of some mysterious character, only claiming that they came from God. To this accusation, the Quranic text responds that in that case, this secret master would have spoken a "barbaric" language, whereas the words spoken by Muhammad are "in clear Arabic": "And certainly We know that they say: Only a mortal teaches him. The tongue of him whom they reproach is barbarous, and this is clear Arabic tongue."[20]

This verse establishes a distinction between Arabic and the language that M. H. Shakir chose to translate as "barbarous." The Arabic word is *ajami*, which signifies "non-Arabic," "foreign," and may also carry a pejorative connotation when used to refer to someone who does not know Arabic or speaks it poorly, or someone whose speech is simply incomprehensible, being derived from a primary meaning of "mute." When it appears in the Quran, it is usually translated as *non-Arabic* or *foreign*. In his translation, Shakir opts for an analogy with the great division effected by the Greeks between those whose language is the Logos itself, reason made language, and those whose idioms exemplified the absence of civilization.

When the Quran says that it is in "clear Arabic tongue," it is not meant to posit a priori the impossibility of its horizontal translation (this would be to declare it incomprehensible, if we are to view "understanding as translation"), but to emphasize that no translation, by definition, is *the*

Quran. A non-Arabic Quran declaring that it is in Arabic is oxymoronic, and one can understand, consequently, why liturgical recitations thereof, which require that it be of *the* Quran, take place in "its" language.

But to contrast a "clear Arabic tongue" with those that are *ajami*, that is to say all other human languages, leads us to understand its sacred status in two different ways. Either the language carries within itself, within its essence, the sacred character that is the reason for its election, or, on the contrary, it was the very fact of welcoming Revelation that rendered it sacred.

In the first case, the divide between the chosen language and all others assumes some attribute that belongs to it and it alone, lacking from the others. An election in this sense would imply, consequently, that some languages are more suitable than others for receiving the word of God, or even for simply discussing prophecies, spiritual truths, etcetera.

In the second case, the "miracle" of vertical translation is explained, on the contrary, as that of the reception of the eternal word by a mere human language, the same as any other. Its sanctity is inscribed in the plurality of equivalent human languages.[21]

## THE *AJAMIZATION* OF THE WORD

It is significant that Lamin Sanneh, speaking of a linguistic "inferiority complex," refers to Arabic, in what is almost certainly a slip of the pen, as the "revealed language of Islam." Such a proposition bears correcting, keeping in mind that it is not the language that is revealed, but the message. Arabic is the language of the Quran. As for being that of Islam, all languages are.

This slip nonetheless points to the existence in the Muslim world of a linguistic ethno-nationalism that holds that the plurality of languages should be organized around a hypercentrality of Arabic and the peripheralization of others, with some languages still more *ajami* than others. African languages in particular, seen through this ethnocentrism as intrinsically pagan, find themselves on the periphery of the periphery.

Among the various possible meanings of the word *ajami*, it has also been used to designate the Persians, even in the pre-Islamic period. With the expansion of Islam and the adoption of the alphabet of the language of the Quran in Muslim societies, it came to signify a non-Arabic literature written with Arabic letters. The expansion of Islam, consequently, led to a "putting in touch" of Arabic with numerous *ajami* (Persian, Turkish, Urdu, Fulani, Mande…), which manifest the hybridizations that these languages went through as a result of translation. Words from the Arabic lexicon are for this reason plentiful in African idioms in which there developed, moreover, specific linguistic registers, resulting in a scholarly and quasi-liturgical use of the language when it is employed to translate and comment on the Quran, to teach theological works, to write mystical poetry…[22]

The works in Wolof of the Senegalese poet Moussa Ka (1889–1963) exemplify this affirmation of the plurality of Islam's languages, setting the movement that Fallou Ngom has called *ajamization*[23] against the ethnocentric model. The following words are oft cited from the mystical poet:

> Let me say this to those who claim that Wolof is unbecoming
> To write verse in Wolof, in dignified language and in any other is all the same
> As they endeavor to praise God's prophet they see their essence ennobled.[24]

What is ultimately at stake is that which is expressed by the work in Wolofal by Moussa Ka.[25] *Ajamization* manifests the value of pluralism by affirming the equal "nobility" of human languages and their continued ennobling through translation. And it is this movement, this particular mode of translating, that is, like the Quranic school, at the heart of the expansion of Islam. For it is not a loss of meaning but its deepening that maintains the word and conserves the "true original" of which Spinoza spoke.

# CONCLUSION:
# THE LANGUAGE OF LANGUAGES

◆

> I am called to take interest in your community, and you to take interest in mine, and we are called to construct and to forge genuine human relationships, not abstract relationships which, in the end, will never be anything more than business relationships.[1]
>
> —JEAN-TOUSSAINT DESANTI

THIS DECLARATION FROM UMBERTO ECO is oft repeated: the language of Europe is translation. The following, from Ngũgĩ Wa Thiong'o, is certainly less proverbial: "Translation is the language of languages, a language through which all languages can talk to one another."[2]

Tiphaine Samoyault rightly described Eco's formula as undoubtedly "efficient" but "false":[3] translation is no more a language than are the automatic *truchements* that allow one to hear in their idiom sentences from another, to which we need not pay any real mind. Such "translation" does not encourage knowing other languages: it replaces it.[4]

As for Ngũgĩ Wa Thiong'o's declaration, not only is it a broadening of Eco's remark toward all of humanity, but it also invites languages not to ignore each other but to "talk" to one another through translation. Through the work of translation, languages come to know each other. From language to language.

The fact that the nationalism of Ngũgĩ Wa Thiong'o, an advocate for African languages in their plurality against linguistic colonialism, is also in praise of translation as understood here should come as no surprise. "Remembering"[5] Africa is a task and a struggle for a unity founded on pluralism. Therein lies the reason behind what one could call his optimism for translation.

The previous pages were dictated by this same optimism for translation, understood according to Antoine Berman's definition as a "putting in touch" of languages. This is why we have encountered this expression several times.

But let us repeat: optimism is not naiveté.

We are not to ignore that this "putting in touch" of languages can be a kiss of death. Indeed, when it comes to the fact that languages can die from the contact among them, *extinct* languages, as they are called, are here, or rather, are no longer here, to bear witness. In this way, in Senegal, the Sénélangues project[6] had reported that the Bapen language was extinct. Today it has completely disappeared. The linguist Adjaratou O. Sall found a woman who still knew a few songs in the language. But they were true swan songs, as the woman in question no longer understood what they meant.

With Bapen, a whole world has left, whisked away by the movement of Wolofization of Senegalese cultures and languages. We can agree that movements of this type exist in the universe of languages, but this is not to say that it still exists in a state of nature governed by the war of all against all. The subdued violence that a language like Wolof, solely by virtue of its nature as a deterritorialized lingua franca, can exert over an idiom made vulnerable by the low number of its speakers is not a counterargument against the ethics of putting languages in touch through translation. On the contrary, the work of translation is one response to the consequences of linguistic domination. Its ethics of reciprocity is likewise a dimension of the political fight against inequality.

No less should we ignore that translation can be ill-intentioned and sometimes appears as a veritable declaration of war. The exemplar thereof is the first Latin translation of the Quran, commandeered and directed by Peter the Venerable, abbot of Cluny. It was no small event when he went to Spain in 1142, the year preceding the work's publication, to meet the team of translators that he had assembled.

First, this date marked the beginning of what the abbot considered himself to be the war against Islam by other, intellectual and, for starters, translational, means. What's more, the undertaking took place in Spain, that is to say in a "translation zone," to use the expression coined by Emily Apter,[7] which demonstrates that while cultural contact can favor translation, it can also turn out to be a form of violence.

Peter the Venerable's work, in which we can see the foundation of what has come to be known as "scholarly Islamophobia," is a heinous translation. The goal thereof, as the abbot explained, was to make readable in Latin the falseness, heresy, and vileness of the original. This only made what he referred to as a matter of "faithfulness" more ironic, when he insisted on the decision to add to his team of *truchements* an authentic "Saracen," who, of course, was named... Muhammad.

Of course, worrying about the "faithfulness" of a translation that, first of all, "conveys" in 124 suras a text that contains 114 can hardly resist caricature.

We can indeed say that such a translation is a betrayal, not in the sense of *traduttore traditore*, but because it betrays what the ethics of translation tells us it should be: *principle of charity*, per Quine, *respect*, per Appiah. Consequently, the answer to a violent translation is a hospitable translation. In contrast with the abhorrent work of Peter the Venerable are all the later translations of the Quran into European languages, whose concern for being faithful lay in a true concern for knowing the other. That of Jacques Berque into French is an exemplar.[8]

The remedy for violent translation is translation, because the remedy for dispersion into clans and tribes is humanity.

This dispersion is presented in the biblical myth of Babel as the result of the collapse of a tower constructed by man's hubris, which likewise marked the end of a humanity united by one sole Adamic language. The Quran does not contain this myth of Babel, and the differences among clans and tribes are on the contrary taken as a given. Verse 49:13 of the Quran says, "We have made you tribes and families that you may know each other." We are, at the outset, tribal in our instinct, naturally drawn toward those who look like us and speak our language, as Bergson reminds us. He also tells us, in the same spirit as this verse, that it is incumbent upon us to achieve an "open society" that decenters the tribe. Humanity is not the object of our nostalgia, but our horizon and our task. If God created tribes, it is up to us to build humanity.

For this task, of course, translation is not sufficient, but it is a contribution.

It is not sufficient, since moving from ethno-nationalisms to humanity also presupposes battling the forces of dissociation that are inequalities. Jean Jaurès led one such struggle, that of socialism, when proclaiming "humanity." In the same vein, Léopold Sédar Senghor, champion of "the civilization of the universal" that he was, said that we are called to fight, in particular, against the fault line that he called "the order of injustice that reigns over the relationship between the North and South," which he described as being cultural before being economic, based on "contempt." Incidentally, do we not today have one more example thereof in the injustice of vaccines in our world stricken by COVID?

But translation contributes to the task of achieving humanity, and even better: it identifies with it. And precisely because its project is that of opposition to "apartheid" in order to open tribes up to the knowledge of one another, because it is "the operation by which cultures [. . .] become foreign to themselves, differentiating themselves from themselves—foreign to the rigid images they make of themselves [. . .]"[9] Decentering oneself in order to be open to the principle of humanity effectively makes "the experience of the foreign" worth it. And as a Heptapod leaving Earth, after getting to know us, of course, might have said, reading our classics: *Sic itur ad astra*.

# ACKNOWLEDGMENTS

In 2015, I was invited by the Frobenius Institute of the University of Frankfurt to give, in English, every Monday from April 20 to June 1, a series of lectures on the theme of "translation." These "Jensen Memorial Lectures" provided the material for this work. I would like to thank professors Karl-Heinz Kohl, Mamadou Diawara, and the entire team at the institute for their invitation and their hospitality. I would also like to thank the Institute of Advanced Studies of Nantes, which welcomed and supported the work of transforming these lectures into a book, which is likewise greatly indebted to Peter Connor, with whom I regularly teach a seminar on the philosophy of translation at Columbia. To Peter and to our students I express all my gratitude. Thank you, finally, to Barbara Cassin, alongside whom I have been walking in the field she has opened of the "untranslatables."

# NOTES

## PREFACE TO THE ENGLISH-LANGUAGE EDITION

1 When at last the Cubs won the World Series in 2016, we had moved east eight years before and made New York our new home.

2 John McWhorter, *The Language Hoax: Why the World Looks the Same in Any Language* (New York: Oxford University Press, 2014), 56.

## INTRODUCTION: TRANSLATION AGAINST DOMINATION

1 Antoine Berman, *The Experience of the Foreign: Culture and Translation in Romantic Germany*, trans. S. Heyvaert (Albany: State University of New York Press, 1992), 4.

2 Martin Heidegger, *On the Way to Language*, trans. Peter D. Hertz (New York: Harper and Row, 1982), 57. This quotation, in French translation, can be found in Antoine Berman, *La Traduction et la lettre, ou l'auberge du lointain* [Translation and the letter, or sheltering the far-off] (Paris: Seuil, 1999), 16.

3 Janice Deul, "Opinie: Een witte vertraler voor poëzie van Amanda Gorman: onbegrijpelijk" [Opinion: A white translator for Amanda Gorman's poetry: incomprehensible] *de Volkskrant*, February 25, 2021.

4 Christine Lombez, *La Seconde profondeur. La traduction poétique et les poètes traducteurs en Europe au XX^e siècle* [Second depth. Poetry translation and poet-translators in 20th century Europe] (Paris: Les Belles Lettres, 2016), xv.

5 I allude here to Barbara Cassin's work *Éloge de la traduction* [In praise of translation] (Paris: Fayard, 2016), as well as to the title Leyla Dakhli gives, in *La Vie des idées* [The life of ideas], to her review of François Ost's book *Traduire. Défense et illustration du multilinguisme* [Translating: A defense and demonstration of multilingualism] (Paris: Fayard, 2009): "Le Multilinguisme est un humanisme" ["Multilingualism is a humanism"]. Review accessed July 29, 2021, https://laviedesidees.fr/Le-multilinguisme-est-un-humanisme.html.

6 Pascale Casanova, *La Langue mondiale. Traduction et domination* [The global language: Translation and domination] (Paris: Seuil, 2015).

7 Pascale Casanova thus cites (*La Langue mondiale*, 11) Abram de Swaan's presentation of "the hierarchical constellation of languages" that he lays out in his work *Words of the World: The Global Language System* (Cambridge, UK: Polity Press, 2001), 4–7.

8 Casanova also writes that "those who, collectively, use two languages are the dominated" (*La Langue mondiale*, 129).

9 Gisèle Sapiro, *Translatio: Le marché de la traduction en France à l'heure de la mondialisation* [Translatio: The French translation market in the time of globalization] (Paris: CNRS Éditions, 2016).

10 Casanova, *La Langue mondiale*, 15.

11 Chapter 4 returns to these "absences."

12 In reality, Senghor speaks of the "new Negro," borrowing the expression from the African American philosopher of the Harlem Renaissance Alain Locke. But the remark is much more universal and concerns the human in general.

13 A written version of this speech is published under the title "Le Problème culturel en AOF" [The cultural problem in French West Africa] in *Liberté*, vol. 1, *Négritude et humanisme* [Negritude and humanism] (Paris: Seuil, 1964).

### 1. THE LINGUIST, THE NATIVE, AND THE EXTRATERRESTRIAL

1 Willard Van Orman Quine, *Word and Object* (Cambridge, MA: MIT Press, 1960), 59.

2 Quine discusses this issue at length in the second chapter of *Word and Object*.

3 See Jean-Jacques Rousseau's "Essay on the Origin of Languages," available in one of several English translations in *The Collected Writings of Rousseau*, vol. 7, *Essay on the Origin of Languages and Writings Related to Music*, trans. John T. Scott (Hanover, NH, and London: University Press of New England, 1998), in which he suggests that the first language would have been sung, largely in "imitative sounds," rather than spoken.

4 George Steiner, *After Babel: Aspects of Language and Translation* (New York: Oxford University Press, 1975).

5 Quine, *Word and Object*, 25.

6 Quine, *Word and Object*, 25.

7 Quine writes, "I hold further that the behaviorist approach is mandatory. In psychology, one may or may not be a behaviorist, but in

linguistics one has no choice. Each of us learns his language by observing other people's verbal behavior and having his own faltering verbal behavior observed and reinforced or corrected by others." Willard Van Orman Quine, *Pursuit of Truth* (Cambridge, MA: Harvard University Press, 1992), 37–38.

8 "In my thought experiment," Quine writes, "the 'source language,' as the jargon has it, is Jungle, the 'target language' is English." In *Pursuit of Truth*, 38.

9 Quine, *Word and Object*, 26.

10 Quine, *Pursuit of Truth*, 45.

11 Quine, *Pursuit of Truth*, 47–48.

12 Chapter 4 returns to this point at length.

13 George Boole, *An Investigation of the Laws of Thought* (New York: Dover, 1854), 25.

14 Gottlob Frege, *Posthumous Writings*, trans. P. Long and R. M. White (Hoboken, NJ: Wiley-Blackwell, 1991), 6.

15 Laugier's book *L'Anthropologie logique de Quine. L'Apprentissage de l'obvie* [Quine's logical anthropology: Learning the obvious] (Paris: Vrin, 1992) is, as it happens, dedicated to this crucial dimension.

16 Lucien Lévy-Bruhl, *Ethics and Moral Science*, trans. Elizabeth Lee (London: Archibald Constable and Co., 1905), 57.

17 Lévy-Bruhl, *Ethics and Moral Science*, 55.

18 Lévy-Bruhl, *Ethics and Moral Science*, 55.

19 Lévy-Bruhl, *Ethics and Moral Science*, 56 (translation modified).

20 Lévy-Bruhl, *Ethics and Moral Science*, 59 (translation modified).

21 Lévy-Bruhl, *Ethics and Moral Science*, 61 (translation modified).

22 Quine, *Word and Object*, 77.

23 Quine, *Word and Object*, 53. In a note, Quine indicates that Malinowski had the honesty to modify the translation of remarks gathered from the islanders he studied rather than imputing upon them illogicality or prelogicality.

24 Bruno Ambroise effectively demonstrates the practical end of "the decline of the idea of independent meaning," that each language grasps according to its particular rules, which "would not lead to a lack of understanding of the other, but rather to a sort of ethics of (or in) translation." See Bruno Ambroise, "L'Impossible trahison. Signification et indétermination de la traduction chez Quine" [The

impossible betrayal: Meaning and indetermination of translation in Quine] in *Noesis* 13 (2008): 61–80.

25 This expression, mentioned by Quine, for example, in section 13 of chapter 2 of *Word and Object*, which we owe to Neil L. Wilson, was primarily used by Donald Davidson.

26 Denis Bonnay and Sandra Laugier, "La Logique sauvage de Quine à Lévi-Strauss" ["Savage logic from Quine to Lévi-Strauss"], in *Archives de philosophie* 66, no. 1 (2003): 64.

27 Ted Chiang, *Stories of Your Life and Others* (New York: Vintage Books, 2002).

28 In an interview published in *The Believer* (no. 128, December 2, 2019), Chiang indicates that his body of work consists in "finding ways to make philosophical questions storyable," adding that "dramatizing these philosophical questions is a way of making their relevance clearer to people."

29 Chiang, *Stories of Your Life and Others*, 121.

30 Chiang, *Stories of Your Life and Others*, 127.

31 Henri Bergson, *Les Deux sources de la morale et de la religion*, (Paris: Presses universitaires de France, 1976 [1932]). Available in English as *The Two Sources of Morality and Religion* (New York: Henry Holt and Co., 1935).

## 2. THE *TRUCHEMENT* AND THE TRANSLATOR

1 Aimé Césaire, "Genève et le monde noir" [Geneva and the Black world], in Annick Thébia-Melsan, ed., *Aimé Césaire pour regarder le siècle en face* [Aimé Césaire to face the century head-on] (Paris: Maisonneuve et Larose, 2000), 27.

2 Amadou Hampâté Bâ, *Vie et enseignement de Tierno Bokar. Le Sage de Bandiagara* (Paris: Seuil, 1980). Available in English as *A Spirit of Tolerance: The Inspiring Life of Tierno Bokar*, trans. Fatima Jane Casewit (Bloomington, IN: World Wisdom, 2008).

3 The colonial administration divided the territory to be managed into "circles" placed under the authority of "commanders."

4 The interrogation and final judgment are found on page 89 of Hampâté Bâ, *A Spirit of Tolerance* (translation modified).

5 Hampâté Bâ, *A Spirit of Tolerance*, 90 (translation modified).

6 A "Picrocholine war," from François Rabelais's *Gargantua*, refers to an absurd, sometimes humorous, conflict with obscure or petty motives. —Tr.

7 Thomas Macaulay, "Minute on Indian Education," in Bill Ashcroft, Gareth Griffiths, and Helen Tiffin, eds., *The Postcolonial Studies Reader* (New York: Routledge, 1994).

8 Macaulay, "Minute on Indian Education."

9 Yves Citton contrasts the "dream of a medium that would be a perfectly transparent *intermediary*, capable of 'transmitting without transforming' in any way what passes through it" and what Bruno Latour calls a *mediator*, which Citton summarizes as "the agent of a process of communication where one cannot transmit without transforming." He adds, "The mediator usually intervenes in a conflict situation, where belligerents are sending each other bombs as messages. The mediator must therefore not only transform messages, translating them from one language to another, but must be able (if necessary) to lie a little or discreetly twist the truth, so as to bring his or her enemies to the bargaining table, and then to a peace agreement." See Yves Citton, *Mediarchy*, trans. Andrew Brown (Cambridge, UK: Polity Press, 2019).

10 Homi Bhabha, *The Location of Culture* (London and New York: Routledge, 2004 [1994]), 55.

11 Here I have adopted the word many use to mean "oral literature."

12 Ralph Austen dedicates the article "Interpreters Self-Interpreted: The Autobiographies of Two Colonial Clerks" to these important auxiliaries of the colonial administration. See Ralph Austen, "Interpreters Self-Interpreted: The Autobiographies of Two Colonial Clerks," in Benjamin N. Lawrence, Emily Lynn Osborn, and Richard L. Roberts, eds., *Intermediaries, Interpreters, and Clerks: African Employees in the Making of Colonial Africa* (Madison: University of Wisconsin Press, 2006).

13 Antoine Berman has written that "we should *study* all the key words that serve to define, in each language, the act of translating, its forms, its demands, etc. Starting with those which refer to translation itself: translation, *traduction*, *Übersetzung*, etc." See Antoine Berman, *La Traduction et la lettre, ou l'auberge du lointain* [Translation and the letter, or sheltering the far-off] (Paris: Seuil, 1999), 74. Here, I would remark that the word I used, *transvasement* [lit. "decanting," to pour from one vessel to another—Tr.], is *sotti* in Wolof, which also signifies "to translate" in that language. Another word in that language meaning "to translate" is *tekki*, which literally means "to unknot, to untie" (*dénouer*), and which implies that translation,

in the target language, undoes the manner in which meaning and words are intertwined in the source language. The same can be said of a third word, *firi*, another rendering of "to translate," and which literally means "to undo braids."

14 Léopold Sédar Senghor and Abdoulaye Sadji, *La Belle histoire de Leuk-le-Lièvre* [The great story of Leuk the Hare] (Paris: Hachette, 1953).

15 Bernard Dadié, *Le Pagne noir: Contes africains* (Paris: Présence Africaine, 1955). Available in English as *The Black Cloth: A Collection of African Folktales*, trans. Karen C. Hatch (Amherst: University of Massachusetts Press, 1987).

16 Birago Diop, *Les Contes d'Amadou Koumba* (Paris: Présence Africaine, 1947), available in English as *Tales of Amadou Koumba*, trans. Dorothy S. Blair (London: Oxford University Press, 1966), and *Les Nouveaux Contes d'Amadou Koumba* [New tales of Amadou Koumba] (Paris: Présence Africaine, 1958).

17 Ralph Austen, "Africans Speak, Colonialism Writes: The Transcription and Translation of Oral Literature Before World War II," in *Discussion Papers in the African Humanities* (Boston: Boston University African Studies Center, 1990), 2.

18 François-Victor Équilbecq, *Essai sur la littérature merveilleuse des Noirs suivi de Contes indigènes de l'Ouest africain français* [Essay on the Marvelous Black Literature, followed by Native Tales of French West Africa] (Paris: Ernest Leroux, 1913).

19 Équilbecq, *Essai sur la littérature merveilleuse des Noirs*, i.

20 Austen, "Africans Speak, Colonialism Writes," 3.

21 Lamin Sanneh, *Translating the Message: The Missionary Impact on Culture*, 2nd ed. (New York: Orbis, 2015).

22 Ralph Austen writes, "Where missionary colonialism most clearly intervenes in shaping the literature . . . is in both the construction of texts compatible with Christian conceptions and the omission of much which conflicts with such values. The construction is most significant in the proliferation of 'creation myths' that emphasize the monotheistic dimension of African belief." Austen, "Africans Speak, Colonialism Writes," 4.

23 Here I paraphrase Antoine Berman, who writes, "There is a tinge of the violence of cross-breeding in translation." Berman, *The Experience of the Foreign: Culture and Translation in Romantic Germany*,

trans. S. Heyvaert (Albany: State University of New York Press, 1992), 4.

24 Christine Le Quellec Cottier, preface to Blaise Cendrars, *Anthologie nègre*, suivi de *Petits Contes nègres pour les enfants des blancs, Comment les blancs sont d'anciens noirs* et de *La Création du monde* [Negro anthology, followed by Little black tales for white children, How whites are former blacks, and The creation of the world] ed. Cottier (Paris: Denoël, 2005), xxv. *Anthologie nègre* available in English as *The African Saga*, trans. Margery Bianco (New York: J. J. Little & Ives, 1927). *Petits Contes nègres pour les enfants des blancs* available in English as *Little Black Stories for Little White Children*, trans. Margery Bianco (New York: Payson & Clarke, ltd., 1929).

25 Cottier, preface to *Anthologie nègre*, xxiii.

26 Cendrars, *African Saga*, 7 (translation modified).

27 Cottier, preface to *Anthologie nègre*, xvi. This reception of "Negro tales" by Blaise Cendrars is analogous to the reception of "Negro art" by such poets and artists as Apollinaire and Picasso. The following chapter returns to this point.

28 Cottier, preface to *Anthologie nègre*, xv.

29 Senghor, preface to Diop, *Les Contes d'Amadou Koumba*, 11–12 [my translation—Tr.].

30 Senghor writes, "However, Birago Diop is not claiming to create an original work; he sees himself as a disciple of the griot Amadou, son of Koumba, whose sayings he is satisfied with translating. But, as we can guess, this is out of modesty. For Birago Diop is not satisfied by working word for word. He has lived the griot's stories, as only black-African listeners know how, and has rethought and written them as a Negro and French artist at the same time, keeping in mind that *traduttore traditore*." Léopold Sédar Senghor, preface to Diop, *Les Nouveaux Contes d'Amadou Koumba*, 7.

31 Jean-Paul Sartre, "Orphée noir," preface to Léopold Sédar Senghor, *Anthologie de la nouvelle poésie nègre et malgache de langue française* [Anthology of new Negro and Malagasy poetry in French] (Paris: Presses Universitaires de France, 1969 [1948]). "Orphée noir" available in English as "Black Orpheus," trans. John MacCombie, *The Massachusetts Review*. 6, no. 1 (Autumn 1964–Winter 1965): 13–52.

32 Berman, *Experience of the Foreign*, 5, 193.

### 3. TRANSLATIONS OF CLASSICAL AFRICAN ART

1 Barbara Cassin and Danièle Wozny, *Les Maisons de la sagesse-traduire: Une nouvelle aventure* [Houses of wisdom-translating: A new adventure] (Paris: Bayard, 2021), 230.

2 Felwine Sarr and Bénédicte Savoy, *Restituer le patrimoine africain* (Paris: Philippe Rey et Seuil, 2018). Available in English as *The Restitution of African Cultural Heritage: Toward a New Relational Ethics*, trans. Drew S. Burk, https://www.about-africa.de/images/sonstiges/2018/sarr_savoy_en.pdf.

3 Bénédicte Savoy, *Africa's Struggle for Its Art: History of a Postcolonial Defeat*, trans. Susanne Meyer-Abich (Princeton, NJ, and Oxford, UK: Princeton University Press, 2021).

4 Cited in Sarr and Savoy, *The Restitution of African Cultural Heritage*, 20.

5 In the original French, Diagne uses both the terms *traduction* and *translation*, the latter of which refers to the geometric sense of translation as well as to the linguistic process of changing a word from one grammatical category to another. —Tr.

6 See Philippe Dagen, *Primitivismes: Une Invention moderne* [Primitivisms: A modern invention] (Paris: Gallimard, 2019), préface.

7 Dagen, *Primitivismes*, préface.

8 Dagen, *Primitivismes*, préface.

9 Joshua Cohen, *The "Black Art" Renaissance: African Sculpture and Modernism Across Continents* (Oakland: University of California Press, 2020), x.

10 Joshua Cohen, "Fauve Masks: Rethinking Modern 'Primitivist' Uses of African and Oceanic Art, 1905–8," *The Art Bulletin* 99, no. 2 (June 2017): 137.

11 Cohen, "Fauve Masks," 137.

12 This story, which Vlaminck recounts in his 1943 *Portraits avant décès* [Portraits before death], is cited at length in Cohen, *The "Black Art" Renaissance*, 26–27.

13 Cohen, *The "Black Art" Renaissance*, 36–37, 75–76.

14 André Malraux, *La Tête d'obsidienne* (Paris: Gallimard, 1974), 17–18. Available in English as *Picasso's Mask*, trans. June Guicharnaud (New York: Holt, Rinehart and Wilson, 1976).

15 The label is applied, from the outside, to the process of these mediators that were the avant-garde poets and artists. In this regard,

Joshua Cohen notes that "primitivism appears nowhere in his [Derain's] writings." Cohen, *The "Black Art" Renaissance*, 50.

16 Appiah responds in this way, in the *New York Times Magazine* (August 22, 2021), in which he regularly holds a column on ethical issues, to a reader worried that he is guilty of cultural appropriation—sign of the times!—for having used aspects of indigenous American cultural practices in a group therapy setting. But what could be a more eloquent mark of respect, Appiah reassures him, than putting these practices in place in order to heal people?

17 Simon Gikandi, "Picasso, Africa, and the Schemata of Difference," *Modernism/Modernity* 10, no. 3 (2003): 455–80.

18 Dagen, *Primitivismes*, 329.

19 William Rubin, *"Primitivism" in 20th Century Art: Affinity of the Tribal and the Modern* (New York: Museum of Modern Art, 1984).

20 Gikandi, "Picasso, Africa, and the Schemata of Difference," 458.

21 Gikandi, "Picasso, Africa, and the Schemata of Difference," 469.

22 Quoted in Malraux, *Picasso's Mask*, 10 (translation modified).

23 Rubin, *Primitivism*, 241–343.

24 Léopold Sédar Senghor, "L'Esthétique négro-africaine" [The Negro-African aesthetic] in *Liberté*, vol. 1, *Négritude et humanisme* (Paris: Seuil, 1964), 211–12.

25 See Souleymane Bachir Diagne, "Musée des mutants" [Museum of mutants], in *Esprit*, no. 406 (July–August 2020): 103–11.

26 Gikandi, "Picasso, Africa, and the Schemata of Difference," 466.

27 During the Algerian War of Independence, the "suitcase carriers" (*porteurs de valises*) were French militants who aided the Algerian National Liberation Front (FLN). —Tr.

28 Paul Ricœur, *On Translation*, trans. Eileen Brennan (London and New York: Routledge, 2006), 5.

29 Ricœur, *On Translation*, 10 (translation modified).

30 This article is quoted in Cohen, *The "Black Art" Renaissance*, 132.

31 The same is true for contemporary artists. If they are descendents of "those who created [an irreplaceable cultural heritage]," they are no less obligated to carry out the work of translating it into the languages of today, so that they may receive it. Speaking of today's Congolese artists, the philosopher Jean-Luc Aka-Evy highlights that their profession is no longer the one that produced the classic art of the region, explaining that it has now become "urban" and "individual." See Jean-Luc Aka-Evy, *Créativité africaine et primitivisme*

*occidental* [African creativity and Western primitivism] (Paris: L'Harmattan, 2018), 197–98.

32 Felwine Sarr and Bénédicte Savoy borrow this word from art historian John Peffer regarding African artifacts torn away from the continent.

**4. THE PHILOSOPHER AS TRANSLATOR**

1 Achille Joseph Mbembe, "Decolonizing the University: New Directions," *Arts and Humanities in Higher Education* 15, no. 1 (2016): 36.

2 Émile Benveniste, "Catégories de pensée et catégories de langue," *Les Études philosophiques* 13, no. 4, (October–December 1958): 419–29. The text is reproduced in Benveniste, *Problèmes de linguistique générale* (Paris: Gallimard, 1966), available in English as "Categories of Thought and Language," *Problems in General Linguistics*, trans. Mary Elizabeth Meek (Coral Gables, FL: University of Miami Press, 1971).

3 Benveniste refers to Ewe as a "language spoken in Togo." In fact, this language is also spoken in the south of Ghana as well as in Benin. We should note that the philosopher Paulin Hountondji of Benin—in an important article dedicated to evaluating Benveniste's examples with the accuracy of someone who knows the language—notes that, in French, it should be spelled "Eve," not "Ewe," which is, he says, "a Germanism inherited from the age of German domination in Togo, *w* being pronounced *v* in German." See Paulin Hountondji, "Langues africaines et philosophie: l'hypothèse relativiste" [African languages and philosophy: The relativist hypothesis], *Les Études philosophiques*, no. 4 (October–December 1982): 393–406. Having made this precision, I nonetheless maintain the spelling *Ewe,* which is still standard, so as to be consistent with Benveniste's text.

4 Benveniste, "Categories of Thought and Language," 57.

5 Benveniste, "Categories of Thought and Language," 57.

6 Benveniste, "Categories of Thought and Language," 61.

7 Friedrich Nietzsche, *Beyond Good and Evil*, in *Basic Writings of Nietzsche*, trans. Walter Kaufmann (New York: The Modern Library, 1968), 217.

8 Benveniste, "Categories of Thought and Language," 62.

9 Jacques Derrida, "The Supplement of Copula: Philosophy *Before* Linguistics," trans. James Creech and Josué Harari, in *The Georgia Review* 30, no. 3 (Fall 1976): 527–64.

10 Derrida, "The Supplement of Copula."

11 Cicero, *De Finibus Bonorum et Malorum* [About the ends of good and evil], book 1, trans. Harris Rackham (London: William Heinemann, 1931), 9.

12 Benveniste, "Categories of Thought and Language," 62.

13 Cited in "To Translate," in Barbara Cassin, ed., *Dictionary of Untranslatables: A Philosophical Lexicon*, trans. edited by Emily Apter, Jacques Lezra, Michael Wood (Princeton, NJ: Princeton University Press, 2014), 1149.

14 Roger-Pol Droit, *Un Voyage dans les philosophies du monde* [A journey through world philosophies] (Paris: Albin Michel, 2021), 16.

15 Droit, *Un Voyage dans les philosophies du monde*, 16. Droit points to "three considerably influential German philosophers, Hegel, Husserl, and Heidegger, who all adopt the same expression: 'only in the Greeks'" (p. 17), as the primary actors behind the "barbed wire" that was put up around "philosophy" as supposedly belonging to the West.

16 Thus does Husserl, in his famous Vienna lecture of 1935, declare that the philosophical essence of Europe demands that India seek to Europeanize itself, as much as it can, while Europe's complete understanding of itself would preclude it from becoming Indianized in the slightest. See Souleymane Bachir Diagne, "Décoloniser l'histoire de la philosophie" [Decolonizing the history of philosophy], in *Cités*, no. 72 (2017).

17 The text is reproduced in French and examined in Abdelali Elamrani Jamal, *Logique aristotélicienne et grammaire arabe* [Aristotelian logic and Arabic grammar] (Paris: Vrin, 1983). I propose an analysis thereof in Souleymane Bachir Diagne, *Open to Reason: Muslim Philosophers in Conversation with the Western Tradition*, trans. Jonathan Adjemian (New York: Columbia University Press, 2018), chap. 2: "How a Language Becomes Philosophical."

18 Jean-Pierre Lefebvre, "Philosophie et philologie: les traductions des philosophes allemands" [Philosophy and philology: Translations of German philosophers], in *Encyclopedia universalis*, symposium "Les Enjeux" [The stakes], vol. 1, 1990, 170.

19 The American anthropologist and linguist Edward Sapir (1884–1939), a specialist in indigenous American languages, was the most staunch defender of the axiom that no language "lacked" anything, and that the idea itself was even contradictory.

20 Diedrich Hermann Westermann (1875–1956), a pioneer in African linguistics, wrote, notably, a grammar of Ewe in 1907.

21 Benveniste, "Categories of Thought and Language," 62. In his article "Langues africaines et philosophie" [African languages and philosophy], 397–98, Hountondji demonstrates "the specious characters of some of the proposed translations" in Benveniste's article and concludes that the "trap that is this kind of comparison [the one established by Benveniste between French and Ewe] not only comes from the minimal violence constituting any translation, but lies above all in the temptation to accentuate or artificially inflate their differences." Hountondji's demonstration is positively enlightening. That said, he concedes that in spite of all that, "the central thesis" of the article remains unaffected. Here, I follow Hountondji's conclusion.

22 Benveniste, "Categories of Thought and Language," 63.

23 Alexis Kagamé, *La Philosophie bantu-rwandaise de l'être* [Bantu-Rwandan philosophy of being] (Brussels: Académie Royale des Sciences Coloniales, 1956). While Abbot Kagamé's thesis was published before Benveniste's article, Hountondji writes that the latter "involuntarily" brings the former's theses a "theoretical caution."

24 Alexis Kagamé, *La Philosophie bantu comparée* [Comparative Bantu philosophy] (Paris: Présence Africaine, 1976), 117–18.

25 Kagamé, *La Philosophie bantu comparée*, 121.

26 Kagamé, *La Philosophie bantu comparée*, 121–22.

27 Hountondji, "Langues africaines et philosophie," 404.

28 *Decolonising the Mind: The Politics of Language in African Literature* (London and Portsmouth, NH: James Currey / Heinemann, 1986) is the title of Ngũgĩ Wa Thiong'o's classic work of decolonial literature, an important book that he describes as his "farewell to English."

29 Kagamé, *La Philosophie bantu comparée*, 126. It is the author who capitalized "Bantu" (which would otherwise be lowercase in French) and "Philosophy," an illustration of his essentialist vision.

30 George Steiner, *After Babel: Aspects of Language and Translation* (New York: Oxford University Press, 1975), 1.

31 She writes, for example, "An 'untranslatable' is a symptom of the differences between languages. Not that one does not translate, but rather, that one never stops translating, or, more precisely, never stops (not) translating. A serious effort is triggered before one is able to find a 'near' analogue, a correspondence in another language. These symptoms, non-exhaustive by definition, allow us to take measure of the differences between texts and therefore between the languages, cultures, worldviews, and religions that they

have at their disposal." Barbara Cassin and Danièle Wozny, *Les Maisons de la sagesse-traduire: Une Nouvelle aventure* [Houses of wisdom-translating: A new adventure] (Paris: Bayard, 2021), 173.

32 On Kwasi Wiredu's philosophical practice, which she calls decolonization-deconstruction, see Séverine Kodjo-Grandvaux, *Philosophies africaines* [African philosophies] (Paris: Présence africaine, 2013): 113–14.

33 Kwasi Wiredu, "The Concept of Truth in the Akan Language," in *Cultural Universals and Particulars: An African Perspective* (Bloomington and Indianapolis: Indiana University Press, 1996).

34 Wiredu, "The Concept of Truth in the Akan Language," 109.

35 Benveniste, "Categories of Thought and Language," 64.

### 5. TRANSLATING THE WORD OF GOD

1 George Steiner, *After Babel: Aspects of Language and Translation* (New York: Oxford University Press, 1975), 250–51.

2 Cheikh Hamidou Kane, *Ambiguous Adventure*, trans. Katherine Woods (New York: Walker and Co., 1963).

3 The spellings *Tierno* and *Thierno* are both acceptable; Amadou Hampâté Bâ uses the former while Cheikh Hamidou Kane uses the latter. —Tr.

4 Kane, *Ambiguous Adventure*, 3.

5 Kane, *Ambiguous Adventure*, 5.

6 Kane, *Ambiguous Adventure*, 4.

7 I examine what I call vertical translation and horizontal translation in my contribution, entitled "Traduire la parole de Dieu" [Translating the word of God], to the exhibition catalog for *Après Babel, traduire* [Translating after Babel] (Arles: Actes Sud et Mucem, 2016), 177–85. Here I take up several elements of that reflection once again.

8 Benedict de Spinoza, *A Theologico-Political Treatise and A Political Treatise*, trans. R. H. M. Elwes (Mineola, NY: Dover Publications, 2004), 165.

9 Spinoza, *A Theologico-Political Treatise*, 165.

10 The expression "neither sound nor letter" to speak of the word of God is common in the language of Islamic philosophy.

11 Al-Ghazali, *Al-Ghazali's "Moderation in Belief,"* trans. Aladdin M. Yaqub (Chicago and London: The University of Chicago Press, 2017), 122.

12 Thus, when verse 4 of chapter 43 declares that "truly, the Mother of the Book remains [forever] before God," this is identified by certain commentators with "the preserved Tablet," per another Quranic expression, from which, as Abdullah Yusuf Ali, who translated the Quran into English, wrote in a footnote to this verse, "are derived all streams of knowledge and wisdom, that flow through Time and feed the intelligence of created minds." See *The Meaning of the Holy Qur'an*, trans. Abdullah Yusuf Ali (Beltsville, MD: Amana Publications, 1989), 1264.
13 Lamin Sanneh, *Translating the Message: The Missionary Impact on Culture*, 2nd ed. (New York: Orbis, 2015).
14 Sanneh, *Translating the Message*, 256–57.
15 Sanneh, *Translating the Message*, 5.
16 Sanneh, *Translating the Message*, 253.
17 Sanneh, *Translating the Message*, 255.
18 Sanneh, *Translating the Message*, 253.
19 *Holy Qur'an*, trans. M. H. Shakir (Elmhurst, NY: Tahrike Tarsile Qur'an, 1983), 26:192–95.
20 *Holy Qur'an*, 16:103.
21 One could consider it to be in this sense that the Quranic text declares that the differences among languages and human colors are among the signs of God (30:22).
22 Tal Tamari has dedicated significant work to these developments. See, for example, the study entitled "L'Enseignement de l'unicité divine expliqué en bambara. Un Commentaire oral sur la *Umm al-Barāhīn* de Muhammad as-Sanūsī" [The teaching of divine unicity explained in Bambara: An oral commentary on Muhammad as-Sanūsī's *Umm al-Barāhīn*], in Jean-Louis Triaud and Constant Hamès, eds., *Isalm et sociétés au sud du Sahara*, vol. 5, *Afrique subsaharienne et langue arabe* [Islam and sub-Saharan societies, vol. 5, Sub-Saharan Africa and Arabic] (Paris: Les Indes Savantes, 2019), 79–218.
23 Fallou Ngom, *Muslims Beyond the Arab World: The Odyssey of 'Ajamī and the Murīdiyya* (Oxford, UK: Oxford University Press, 2016).
24 Fallou Ngom reproduces Moussa Ka's poem entitled "Taxmiis bub Wolof" (The Wolof Takhmīs), "modeled on the classical Arabic poetic form called takhmis structured around five-line verses," in which he celebrates the equality of all languages and reminds us of

the remark in the Quran that "it is because of divine mercy that there is ethnolinguistic diversity." Ngom, *Muslims Beyond the Arab World*, 60–62.

25 *Wolofal* is the name for *ajami* literature in that language.

CONCLUSION: THE LANGUAGE OF LANGUAGES

1 Jean-Toussaint Desanti, "Négritude au-delà," in Annick Thébia-Melsan, ed., *Aimé Césaire pour regarder le siècle en face* [Aimé Césaire to face the century head-on] (Paris: Maisonneuve et Larose, 2000), 55.

2 Ngũgĩ Wa Thiong'o, *Something Torn and New: An African Renaissance* (New York: Basic Civitas Books, 2009), 96.

3 Tiphaine Samoyault, *Traduction et violence* [Translation and violence] (Paris: Seuil, 2020), 19.

4 "Translation would replace knowing others' languages," Samoyault writes in *Traduction et violence*, 19.

5 The Kenyan writer often uses this word to mean "simultaneously," as the different possible meanings of the term allow, an effort for *memory* as well as a movement of *unification*.

6 This is an undertaking of the French CNRS (National Center for Scientific Research) directed by linguist Stéphane Robert and dedicated to the languages of Senegal.

7 Emily Apter, *The Translation Zone: A New Comparative Literature* (Princeton, NJ: Princeton University Press, 2006).

8 In the original French, Diagne quotes the translation by Jacques Berque, where the translation by M. H. Shakir is quoted here. See *Le Coran: Essai de traduction*, trans. Jacques Berque (Paris: Albin Michel, 2002). —Tr.

9 Marc Crépon, "Mémoires d'empire (exploitations, importations, traductions)," in *Transeuropéens* 22 (Spring/Summer 2002): 45–58. Crépon speaks of European cultures. By omitting this adjective in the quotation, I broaden the comment, in the spirit of the author, toward cultures in general. And, like him, I borrow the use here of the concept of *apartheid* from Étienne Balibar in "Le droit de cité ou l'apartheid" [The right to the city or apartheid] in *Nous, citoyens d'Europe* [We, citizens of Europe] (Paris, La Découverte, 2001).